No

Yesterday

A novella

Warren Stoddard II

Copyright © 2021 by Warren Stoddard II

PINE NEEDLE FLOOR
Birmingham, Alabama

ISBN: 978-0-578-80978-6

Cover art and design: Nick Resty

This book is for John Delamater.

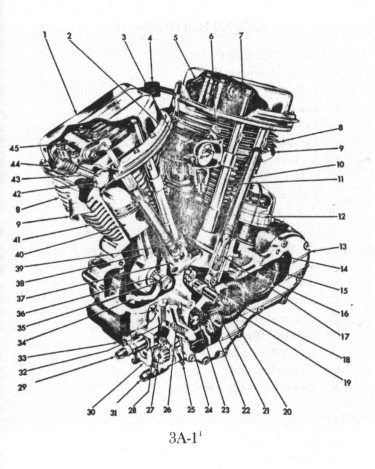

3A-1[1]

[1] "Panhead Engine: Cutaway View." Harley Davidson Panhead Service Manual: 1948-1957 Rigid. Harley-Davison. 1957, pp. 56.

LEGEND FOR FIGURE 3A-1

1. Rocker Arm Cover
2. Cover Reinforcing Ring
3. Carburetor high-speed adjustment
4. Engine mounting bracket
5. Intake valve oiler
6. Carburetor low-speed adjustment
7. Rocker arm
8. Cylinder head
9. Exhaust port
10. Push rod
11. Push rod cover
12. Circuit breaker (timer)
13. Gearcase
14. Generator drive-gear
15. Idler Gear
16. Idler gear spacer
17. Hydraulic lifter
18. Intermediate gear spacer
19. Intermediate gear
20. Tappet and roller assembly
21. Pinion gear
22. Cam gear
23. Breather gear
24. Breather Screen
25. Chain oiler adjustment screw
26. By-pass valve
27. Oil feed pump drive gears
28. Oil Scavenger drive gears

29. Oil return nipple
30. Oil pump
31. Oil feed nipple
32. Check valve
33. Crankcase
34. Flywheel
35. Crankpin
36. Connecting rod roller bearing
37. Tappet guide
38. Connecting rod
39. Tappet adjustment
40. Piston
41. Cylinder
42. Exhaust valve
43. Exhaust valve guide
44. Valve spring
45. Rocker arm bearing

"Señores," said Don Quixote, "let us go slowly, for there are no birds in yesterday's nests. I was mad, and now I am sane; I was Don Quixote of La Mancha, and now I am, as I have said, Alonso Quixano the Good. May my repentance and sincerity return me to the esteem your graces once had for me, and let the scribe continue."

– Miguel de Cervantes: *Don Quixote*

Once that money hits your hand, there's no going back.

The trailers were parked, and the animals grunted and bayed inside as the swirling dust blinded them. Two-by-two, like being unloaded from the Ark, the cattle trotted from the trailers and onto the dusty plains of wide-swaying yellow grass. As they walked they kicked up more dust. It billowed into the air and was lifted higher by the wind. Some of the ruddy brown flecks were cast away on the winds to overtake other pastures and turn them to fallow, barren lands. Some fell softly like red snowflakes backed by blue sky to the earth where particles collected on the boots of the two men, obscuring the patterns, the colors. The ostrich leather of the young man's boots was a subdued brown as he adjusted his stance. He hitched his thumbs in his belt loops. He bit at the inside of his cheek.

The old man flipped through the stack of bills. He licked his forefinger and continued flipping through them until the stack of money was folded in half. The young man opposite him took off his hat and wiped sweat from his brow. He put the wide-brimmed hat back on his head and hitched his thumbs on his belt buckle. The old man unfolded the bills and looked up at the long white trailer the cattle were spilling out of. "Them's good stock?" he asked.

"Nothin' but the very best," answered the young man.

"Like a ranch hand to say that."

"Well I wouldn't say nothin' 'cept for the truth. Old man Hager'd have my backside."

The old man shook his head and felt the weight of the bills in his hand, judging the trailer with his eyes. He smelled of menthol and spat a brown stream of tobacco from his lips. He wiped them with the back of his hand. "Reckon he would," he said as he handed the stack of bills to the young man.

The young man stifled a smile and tucked the money into his back pocket and shook the old man's hand before turning and opening the creaky driver-side door of a rusted F-100 pickup that was once white. He turned the key in the ignition and then rolled down the window of the truck with his left hand; he pulled a pair of aviator sunglasses from the collar of his pearl-snap shirt and put them on before tipping the brim of his hat to the old man and driving away.

Jackson Hunter had just robbed his boss blind. Old men were always getting robbed blind by younger men. First they came for their wives. Then they came for their riches. It wasn't that Hager was a bad guy, or that he deserved it. It was just the way of the world.

Jackson adjusted the knob of the stereo until he picked up the signal of the local country station in Uvalde. The music played softly and the truck purred along smooth now that it had lost the load of cattle. Jackson thought about stopping for a quick lunch in town before he made his getaway. Then he thought that might not be such a good idea on account of the thousands of someone else's dollars he had in his back pocket. People had a way of asking you too many questions when you stopped in for lunch some place in a small town in Texas. "But I am gonna need some gas," he said to himself.

The rolling hills of Uvalde County eventually and suddenly gave way to the Texaco and the shops and the courthouse and the concrete that marked the city of Uvalde from its surrounding countryside. Jackson pulled into the Texaco, pumped his gas and walked into the store and paid the attendant. He walked out the door once, and then walked back in without making eye contact with the attendant and picked a packet of peanuts from one of the shelves. He handed the man seventy-five cents and walked back out the door a second time all without saying a word. The man at the counter gave him a long look as Jackson walked across the parking lot to the gas pumps before sitting back in the chair behind him and flipping through the Wednesday paper.

Sitting in the cab of the truck, Jackson Hunter pulled the stack of bills from his back pocket and began to count. What would you do with it all? He asked himself. *Whatever I want.* This was the money that would change his life. No more ranching. No more Hager. No more dawn till dusk and no more shoveling shit when the outhouse overfilled. He didn't mind Hager. The old man had treated him fair-and-square since the day he turned up on the ranch. Never asked too many personal questions, always paid him on time, and even invited him to supper with his wife some nights.

The old couple never had any kids. Most of their kin was gone too. Maybe Jackson was like that son they never had, or there was some kind of sentimental longing for that kind of connection that Jackson filled. That same day, every day, always be by your side and tell you how they're doing type of connection that the old timers can't get enough of.

They'd tell him stories about the old times when he asked. The pair had been around long enough to remember the turn of the century. Lived in Uvalde all their lives. Born, married, and soon to die here. They'd been on the frontier of the old Wild West in the final years of the glory days.

Jackson loved when they'd tell him stories about the old timers before them. Billy the Kid had come through town one summer on the run from the law, other outlaws hightailed through the prairies to the north. Of course there was always the honorable lawman right on their heels. He'd come through town in the morning on a white horse, wearing a shiny badge, kill the outlaw in a shootout at high noon, and bed the finest eligible bride by sup-pertime. The outlaws feared him. The women wanted his babies. And the boys all hoped one day they'd grow up and be just like him. *Of course, it isn't so easy to be honorable these days.*

Then Jackson got to thinking about what be-ing honorable actually was. Then he wondered whether any of those stories were true about the Old West. Then he thought about the Hagers and all the stories they'd told and everything else they'd done for him. He figured he shouldn't think about that any longer, because he was liable to get to feeling bad about what he was about to do. So he decided it was best to stop thinking altogether. That didn't work. The sky was turning. And just as he was get-ting to feeling bad again he heard the low rumble of two motorcycles pulling up to the pump behind him.

He looked at their reflection in the rearview mirror through the dirty back window. He'd had a motorcycle once before – a little Jap bike that he rode through the bayous of Louisiana in a life that seemed a very long way away from him now – hardly more than a figment of an imagination. That little motorcycle was nothing like the two Harleys that

6

pulled into the Texaco on the third Wednesday morning of January in Uvalde, Texas. These were choppers. At least that's what the guys in Austin called them. He'd seen a few of them on a trip there a couple years back. The ones he'd seen were wild contraptions ridden by the bearded men with death wishes on the outskirts of society. These were no different. They both had long, stretched out front ends that must have doubled the length of the bikes. The rear fenders were chopped off as short as they could be and sissy bars laden with luggage poked into the sky behind the seat. One was yellow, one blue – both outfitted with Panhead engines. It wasn't the latest model of Harley engine, but it had that classic look to it. Jackson got out of the car, walked over without saying hello, and squatted next to the yellow bike. Simple. Clean. Pure. The paint was chipped in places on the frame and the gas tank's colors had faded slightly and cracked from old age. He noticed the way that the yellow of the paint took on a pearlescent orange hue as he squatted down. He looked over the motor and how the fish-tail exhaust pipes both swept out from the heads of the engine and along the line of the frame and then up into the sky beside the rear wheel. He nodded to himself in approval and the owner of the motorcycle eyed him closely.

Jackson noticed the leather-clad man watching him and retreated to the cab of his pickup. He'd left the money bundled in the cupholder. He looked from the bills to the bike to the wild blue open under the Texas sky, down the highway, and up at the roof of the cab of the pickup, and then through the windshield at the Texaco. He thought of the outlaws, of the cowboys, and of the lawmen riding their horses under the beating sun of the Old West. He wondered if the new sun was any hotter or if the stars at night were really as big and bright as they said in the songs.

He looked back at the bikes.

The two riders leaned against their cycles and took slow short drags from cigarettes that dangled loosely from chapped lips. The townspeople entering and exiting the gas station stared at them. They looked like hooligans, or ruffians, or bad news depending on whose conversation you overheard.

Jackson Hunter sat in the cab of Hager's pickup with his head leaning against the back window and his eyes closed. His foot pounded on the floorboard. Eventually, he opened his eyes and grabbed the stack of money and ran a thumb along the edges of the bills so that they made a satisfying ruffling sound like the dealer at a blackjack table – like a gambler about to go all in taking a final moment to enjoy his wealth, his leisure.

He shoved the door of the pickup open wide with his boot, and with all the confidence he could muster, walked up to the man leaning on the yellow bike. "I want it," he said.

Slowly, the man turned from his friend and eyed Jackson. He looked him from his well-worn and faded boots to his blue jeans to his rodeo champion belt buckle, up each of his pearl snaps to his clean-shaved chin, his aviators, and his wide-brimmed ten-gallon hat. The man in the leather jacket breathed a slow cloud of smoke to the side and flicked the cigarette butt to the ground. "You oughtta get back in that truck, cowboy."

"Hell. Trade you for the truck," the cowboy said.

"Trade me for the truck?"

"Straight up."

"Fuck off."

The man on the blue bike rolled his eyes and pulled his helmet over his head. "Let's go," he said to his friend, "fuck this guy."

"The truck and a thousand dollars," Jackson blurted out as the owner of the yellow bike began to do the same.

"Yeah, right," the owner of the yellow bike snorted at him.

Desperate, Jackson reached into his back pocket and shoved the stack of bills out at the man, quickly counting off ten of the 100s. "The truck and a thousand dollars." He shook the smaller bundle of bills.

The man looked at Jackson and down at the money he held in his right hand, then at the larger stack of 100s that he held in his left, and then back to his friend. He turned purposefully to Jackson. "The truck and two thousand," he said suspiciously.

"I get to keep the gear on the back."

"Fine." The man stretched out his open hand and Jackson slapped twenty one-hundred-dollar bills into it, trying to hide the look of surprise on his face.

"Now how do I go about startin' this thing?" Jackson asked.

※※※

The road rushed beneath him now – the grey back of a writhing serpent divided in two by a double yellow line. Wind snapped at his cuffs and the handlebars sliced through the air before him. He leaned back in the seat of the motorcycle with his hands casually holding onto the grips in front of him as though he were reading a book in a rocking chair on the front porch of a locomotive. Jackson Hunter was smiling.

He'd taken the quick starting lesson and then hogged the former owner of the motorcycle for his leather jacket for another hundred dollars.

The unusually hot January afternoon was rendered cool by the self-constructed breeze the motorcycle made howling down the road. The trees whizzed past in a coagulated blur as the yellow Harley scorched through the rising and falling terrain west of Uvalde until their boughs disappeared altogether, and a vast rolling plain of high yellow grass took their place.

He was hell bent on getting as far from Hager's ranch as he could before the old man discovered that his money and his truck weren't coming home. Going north or east would have been too easy, too predictable; the first places they'd search would be San Antonio and Austin, maybe even Victoria. It wasn't Jackson's first rodeo, and he was determined to make it to another. So his escape would be west. He'd go along Highway 90 as far as it took him, then maybe cut up north through New Mexico and bounce back-and-forth from one side of the Continental Divide to the other, or he could hook his route south at the border crossing at Juarez, and then go further south as far as he could, maybe to another continent, maybe to Baja. He heard the surfing was good there, and the cops couldn't bust you even if they wanted to. And surely, with a wad of cash like this in his back pocket, they'd be gunning for him. Hager wouldn't take the loss of his life's work lying down. As it was, the rancher probably stood a better chance of finding Jackson than the *federales* did. He'd have to brush up on his Spanish.

For now, Jackson had nothing but his knees in the breeze and the sun on his face, and so he leaned back against the gear on the back seat and breathed in a deep breath of arid air. Even now, thirty miles outside of Uvalde, he could see the landscape changing. The grass grew in smaller patches and the dirt turned ever redder like the earth was finally bleeding through brown cotton bandages. He felt somehow closer to it, whether that was by proximity to the road in the low-slung seat of the chopper, or that he sensed his own mortality in the claret crust of the continent that seemed to be steadily encroaching on the livelihoods of the foliage, he couldn't be sure.

They'll be after you by the daybreak, he told himself. That was the only thing he could be sure of, so he had to get as far west as he could before the sun set and rose again in the morning. Even that wouldn't be far enough, he thought. Distance becomes irrelevant the deeper into West Texas you go, rendered nothing more than a formality by the vast openness of the desert and the unending honesty of highways that run without a single bend in them, just yellow line and asphalt as far as you can see until it vanishes over the horizon line. As fast as you can get there is how far away "there" is. The rest is all semantics. 150 miles is just the next town over. And everybody knows everybody.

The cops would be hard on his heels. Hager had a reputation for being tighter than a bull's ass at fly time with his money. He was *not* going to let it go that easy, Jackson thought.

But for now, now he was riding. Jackson's mind looped and looped about the same sequence of things until he stopped for gas the first time. And again until he stopped for gas the second time, where the cashier gave him some grief about having to make change for a one-hundred-dollar bill.

"You gonna take my money or not?" Jackson snapped.

The cashier took the money and placed it under the tray in the cash register and set to counting out 97 dollars and 32 cents in change. Jackson pocketed the change and asked where the next filling station was.

"Not till Del Rio, I don't think."

Jackson raised his eyebrows. "Not till Del Rio? Is it far?"

"Yessiree. If I's you I'd get me a gas can to strap on that there contraption of yours. Otherwise yer liable to find yerslef a-pushin', and it is *un*sea-sonably warm for mid-January. Sweat right through that leather jacket, you will."

Jackson agreed and paid the man for a gas can and walked outside to fill it, then walked back inside to pay for the gas, back out to the bike only to realize that he had no way of securing the gas can to the sissy bar and stomped back towards the door of the gas station. "I *ain't* coming back in here again," he said as he entered the doors for the third time and looked around for some bungee cords. There weren't any by the candy, and none near the chips or the beer, but he did find some duct tape next to the 59-cent breakfast burritos, and duct tape would do.

"How are you gonna get it off?" the man behind the counter asked.

Jackson groaned and asked if there was any rope in the store. The man pointed towards some and Jackson retrieved and paid for it, walked out of the store and to his bike before the attendant could ask if he'd rather have bungee cord, wrapped the rope around the gas can and the sissy bar a couple of times, tied several knots, gave it a satisfied shrug, zipped up his jacket, kick-started the bike, and took off down Highway 90 again.

It wasn't long before Jackson passed another gas station. "Sonofabitch tricked me," he said to himself. The little red canister smacking against the sissy bar behind him was a total waste. Maybe it would come in handy later. He just wished it would sit still. The thing's waving about in the wind worked the bike all over the road, and the thumping from behind him each time the wind buffeted the canister was driving Jackson mad; every now and then it would smack the back of his head, compounding the issue.

The sun was setting ahead of him in the western sky now. The little whispers of clouds just above the horizon line were dyed red and purple as the ball of light passed behind them. Over his head the sky faded from red to orange to blue to deep purple like an artist had taken a brush and smeared the paint from one horizon to the next. A sign read: 14 Del Rio.

Fourteen miles to go.

Another smack from the gas can.

He'd need to find a motel for the night, preferably one that wouldn't ask for his name. Maybe he needed an alias; something wild and heroic, a name befitting of an outlaw on the run. A name for a *good* outlaw, he thought. The kind from the movies and the radio shows. Like *Gunsmoke*. He recoiled, reconsidered; the alias should be the opposite. You should choose a name nobody would expect any trouble from, he told himself, nothing to notice; you are just a simple vagabond heading to California on your Harley to join all the hippies in San Francisco, maybe see some Dead concerts. It should be a simple name, one easy enough to remember, but so simple that it would get mixed in with the jumble of other words in the head of whoever was trying to do the remembering. No Harold, or Travis, or Gideon, or Festus; too unique, those would get you caught. No John, or Mark, or Luke; they were too biblical. Those would get you to Hell, a deeper circle of it anyway.

"Dad gummit!" he yelled as the gas can hit his head again. The rattling was impossible to ignore as he rolled through the city limits of Del Rio. It shook the sissy bar, jerking the bike to and fro with the wind. The can was shuddering the whole machine, and all of a sudden it wasn't. And Jackson heard the dreadful thumping of the full can tumbling down the road behind the bike, followed by a screech of tires and the long blaring of a honking horn. There was probably a middle finger aimed his direction too. Jackson looked behind him and saw headlights in a cloud of dust shining off into the brush on the side of the road. It was best to make himself scarce.

He rapped on the throttle and the power of the bike jetted from rear to front so rapidly and with so much force that it pulled the bike onto one wheel, and the front end lifted high into the ten-o-clock position before whamming back down to the pavement and ripping away down the street. He hung a quick left between two Chevys with their horns blaring and roared away down a new road.

The dying light of the sky was the deep blue-gray of a roiling sea, and the buildings and street lamps were nothing but harsh black silhouettes against the final embers of the sun on the horizon until the street lamps snapped and buzzed to life with that same pale electric blue light of the mosquito-killer lamps that hung from the awning of the back porch on the Hager's ranch that would hiss each time an unlucky bug flew lustfully into the pounding blue radiance of the light. The "Live Nude Girls" signs glowed blue too, and the cracks in the road jarred Jackson in his seat. He turned into the blue-washed parking lot of a strip mall and shut his bike off under the florescent false suns of the lamps overhead. He listened to the engine slowly ticking as it cooled, and then he got out of the saddle and walked into a bowling alley.

He ordered his food at the bar and sat alone at a four-seat table. On the lanes, the balls rolled loudly on the wood and sent the pins clattering into the back wall, and a young kid would bend over from behind the curtain and set the knocked-over pins out of the way. The kids rolling the heavy balls loudly down the oiled lane would giggle when they knocked over the pins and their parents would grin and release long drafts of cigarette smoke into the air. The smoke hung heavy from the ceiling of the bowling alley and it made the cheeseburger Jackson bit into taste acrid and addictive, and he longed for fresh air and wondered what the sun was doing on the horizon. By now, it would be nothing more than a pile of embers sitting somewhere on the other side of the Rio Grande, and the horizon out across the northern reaches of Mexico would be barely illuminated, and the clouds that the sun had left behind would look like wind-blown ashes from the fire of the sunset. The world would be turning black and stars would start to pop themselves forth from the blanket of night like moles on the prairie.

The children's legs would show themselves from behind the curtains every so often and their arms would stack the pins neatly after the children on the other end of the lane had thrown the heavy balls of resin down the oiled planks of wood and giggled and looked to their parents for approval. The parents would breathe long breaths of smoke into the air and the smoke would hang low and dense from the ceiling. And they would all be quietly suffocating as the pins clattered and the balls rolled loudly on the oiled wood of the lane and the children giggled and the parents clapped and grinned and breathed their smoke until it hung low from the ceiling and dampened the cacophony of frivolity and Americana on the inside of the bowling alley. Jackson longed for fresh air as he took another bite of the cheeseburger, now less acrid from the dense smoke, but the tomatoes were old, and the patty of the burger was still a little cold in the middle, and the cheese tasted processed and nothing at all like what cheese should taste, and Jackson furrowed his brow and grimaced in disgust.

I am not a good man, he thought.

By now the sky was completely dark outside, and if some man was placed in the middle of the Del Rio night by God himself and had never lived a day other than this night in his life he would never know that the streets did not belong there, and that the town did not belong there, and that the bowling alley where the children and the parents played and laughed and worked and slowly suffocated was never meant to be placed here in the middle of a vast and open desert, and that the stars could out-shine even the false-suns of the street lamps that hung over his head if they were given the chance.

Jackson finished the burger, warmer in the second half than in the middle, and the tomato was not big enough to cover the entire patty so its rancid taste was gone, but still there was the processed cheese that tasted nothing like what cheese should taste. He saw a boy poke his face from behind the curtain as he was standing the pins neatly in a trian-gle and look out longingly at the girl who just rolled the ball down the oiled wooden planks of the lane. She turned and looked proudly at her mother, who was watching her long plume of smoke rise into the dense cloud that hung low from the white-washed ceiling of the bowling alley.

What have we become? Jackson sipped his soda and leaned his chair backwards, lifting the two front legs of it from the checkered tile floor. Maybe none of us are good men anymore. The nature of it all has been molested. Life should not be so *comfortable*. He dropped the front legs of the chair back down to the tile floor and lifted them again, rocking slowly back and forth while he sipped his soda.

He remembered the gut-wrenching jerk of the motorcycle as it lifted vertically. A motorcycle does nothing but run straight down the road. A man is no different, Jackson thought. He will do what is the next logical step in a centuries-long list of tasks that his race has been bound to accomplish until he winds up in a cacophonous bowling alley feeling the heavy cloud of thick smoke press in on him from the whitewashed ceiling above. But when the motorcycle breaks course, when the man breaks course, when they lift vertical in one gut-wrenching motion and the rider can see nothing but the smeared colors of the sky and the first few twinkling stars hanging there in that twilight just before the suns of street-lamps snap to light in the darkness, and the stars are staring down at you as you look helplessly up in weightless freefall, when the front end comes crashing back down to the road and the motorcycle is still going straight down it, you begin to see the world in a more complete way. He longed for fresh air.

Jackson stood and walked to the exit of the building, and as the doors swung shut behind him, all the balls rolling on the oiled wood planks of the lane, and the clattering of the pins, and the giggles of the children, and the clapping of the parents began to fade away, replaced by humming stillness. He breathed in the cold, clean night air under the light of the lamps above him and longed for darkness too.

※ ※ ※

He checked in under an Alias. The motel room that he rented was warm, and probably teeming with an untold number of unseen bugs. He set his keys and knife on the bedside table, undressed and let the shower run. He stared at himself in the mirror. He got in the shower, and once he was clean he got out and wrapped a towel around his waist and lay on top of the covers of the stiff mattress still sopping wet. He stared at the blank ceiling. Then he remembered the bike.

He jumped to his feet and ran out the door to the motorcycle. Stares from silhouettes smoking cigarettes on the upper balcony followed the man dressed only in a plain white towel as he lifted the cycle off its kickstand and began to push. He could feel the stabbing coldness of the rough ground beneath his bare feet. He rolled the Harley up onto the breezeway and through the door to his room. When he had the bike situated and the door closed, his teeth were chattering. He took another hot shower.

He stood in front of the mirror after he got out again and wiped a swathe of the glass clean of steam so that he could see the reflection of himself. Some of the water coagulated into larger droplets on the face of the glass and streaked across the reflection of a face that he could barely recognize as his own. Its familiar lines and features were mutilated by the water on the glass and his hair was unkempt.

His usually clean-shaven face had the hard prickles of five-o-clock shadow peppered over his jawline. There was still the scar on his shoulder from something he could not remember. He stared into his own eyes. They were still the same, the one thing that will never change on a person so long as they live. The familiarity of his eyes bored into him.

They hardly recognized who he was. A good man no longer.

And so he was not. By his own admission, he was a terrible man, the lowest of the low. Scum. Thief. They could call him what they would. He had stolen somewhere in the neighborhood of 10,000 dollars from Hager. In return, Hager had lost over two hundred head of cattle and the best – the only – rancher on his farm.

By now, Hager was sure to be worried. He'd be sitting on that rocking chair on his front porch with a can of beer in his left hand, his face illuminated by the pale blue glow of the mosquito zapper. The boards of the porch would creak as he rocked. He would either be very worried or very angry. But eventually he would know what happened, enough people had seen Jackson parked and eating peanuts at the gas station before he left town. They'd probably seen him take off on the bright yellow Harley too, or heard him if they hadn't seen. Jackson was glad he brought it inside the motel room.

He walked past the bike to the window and peeked out the blinds into the parking lot and counted the cars. Four. No cops.

He wasn't sure how long it would take the old man to figure he'd been swindled out of everything. "I reckon you got 24 hours if yer lucky, give or take," Jackson muttered to himself as he paced the room. Hager'd be rocking in that chair tonight, though. He'd look over his fields until the wife came out to call him to bed. And he'd get up and go to sleep.

Tomorrow Jackson would head northwest; he couldn't cross the border yet. He had to get out of the Valley first. Everyone knew everyone here. But then again, every town from Del Rio to El Paso would be like that. Hopefully he could make some friends.

He dried off and lay down on the unsoaked half of the bed, staring at the picture of an old Spanish mission on the wall. Quaint. Then he rolled onto his back and switched off the lamp and stared at the ceiling. The room was illuminated by a thin sliver of pale light that came in from the parking lot and shone silver moonlight on the motorcycle's gas tank. The ceiling was blank and white and peppered with little pellets to muffle the sound. It was like all the other ceilings he'd seen before, but this one was not rotting, and there was no thick cloud of smoke hanging from it, but the sheets of the bed smelled faintly of cigarettes and felt rough and threadbare to the touch.

Was this how the outlaws did it? Ride all day chasing the sun to settle down in a warm and worn out bedroom? Maybe they snuggled up to their favorite whore in town instead. Maybe they sat around the campfire with their band. A meal would be smoking over the fire and the horses would be grazing nearby. The flames would illuminate their faces and they'd tell stories of the glory days or the good days or maybe just the easy days – the days where they didn't have to worry about money or women or running from the local law. No sheriff on their heels, just a wide open expanse of desert and a good horse on a cool day. There would be no fights, or shootouts, or drunken barroom brawls, or worry about the law. Just ride. Ride as far as you like and if you don't like the way you're headed you can turn right around and start in a new direction all over again. That's the beauty of it.

Here he was, barely an outlaw at all. He'd fought no one to earn this; it was just swindled from an unsuspecting victim. Hadn't been on the run more than a single day and he already regretted what he'd done. But sometimes you just cast your lot in life, he told himself. Sometimes you just cast your lot in life and you got to stick with it. And you've chosen a certain way of living that don't get along with modern society. You've chose it and that's all there is to it. You've chosen to be the kind of man that you are now. Chose it and you got to stick with it. What were you going to tell Hager anyway? You'd gotten a flat tire so you decided to up and buy this yellow motorcycle with *his* money and trade away *his* truck just so you could get the 10 miles home? Then you somehow got lost on the way and showed up late to work the next day to boot? No. Now you are an outlaw and because of the things you've done you have to accept that you're an outlaw and you'd best live up to this ideal you've got in your head of being a fugitive from the law. You'd best live up to this lifestyle that you chose or you won't have much living left to do. You're in it now. Too deep to get out. You'll go west tomorrow and you won't miss Hager's ranch or your bed or your childhood. This is who you are now. This is who you've become, and you've become it by your own accord, so you'd best make the most of it, because it's the only thing in this world that you got.

Jackson fell asleep dreaming of the easy days.

❋ ❋ ❋

When he woke a woman was beating on his back with a wadded-up towel, screaming in broken English. "No motorcycle in room. I call police!" Jackson threw his hands up and rolled off the bed away from the woman. "You stain carpets! I call police! I tell manager." She scooted around the bed toward Jackson and he jumped up onto the mattress wearing nothing but boxer shorts. "I call police," she shrieked.

"No police," Jackson said, putting his palms up towards the woman. "No *federales.*"

"I call police!"

"No police. Calm down."

"I tell manager! ¡*Le dire a mi gerente*!"

"No manager. No police. *Nada*. No *federales* neither. *Amigos*, you and me."

The woman bolted toward the door and Jackson hopped down onto the floor and stood in her way. "No," he said. He put his palms up toward her and she swung the heavy towel at him. It must have been loaded with some weight, because it sent him backwards into the wall. The woman stepped through the doorway, but Jackson recovered and grabbed her by the arm. He threw her into the room and onto the bed. The woman sent a bloodcurdling yell out the door and into the brightness of the South Texas morning. Jackson straddled over the top of her and shoved his hand over her mouth. She was still writhing and jerking beneath him. Jackson grabbed his knife from the bedside table and unsheathed it – he pressed the razor edge of the blade to the woman's throat. "Shut the fuck up or I'll kill you," he snarled. The woman went silent and Jackson reached for the drawer behind him and grabbed two bills from it. "Take this money. Do not call the police. Understand? *Comprende*?"

The woman stared with wide white eyes back at him like a deer caught in the headlights of an eighteen-wheeler. "I'll blow you off this fucking planet if you talk to the police. I will run you down, and I will kill you. I will push this knife into your fucking throat, and you will die because you couldn't keep your goddamned mouth shut. Understand?" His voice was low and graveled. She nodded with tears in her eyes. He lifted the knife from her throat and eased the pressure of his hand off the woman's face and stood from the bed. The woman looked at the bills and tucked them in her bra before she too stood from the bed and bolted through the door, leaving her cleaning cart in the breezeway.

"Shit." Jackson pulled on the same pants and pearl-snap shirt he was wearing the day before and stomped his feet into his boots. He pushed the motorcycle out the door of the room and into the parking lot as quickly as he could. He kick-started the bike and as it warmed he looked at the motel and saw at least a half dozen of the burgundy curtains pulled askew with heads and eyes of inquisitive strangers staring at him standing next to the yellow chopper with the sissy bar and the upswept exhaust, and he wearing his aviators and a leather jacket, with a face that hadn't been shaved in two days, and his brown cowboy boots that stood on the asphalt of the motel parking lot in the midmorning sun. He wished he'd woken sooner. The sun was bright. One of the curtains silently swung closed behind the window, and Jackson figured he ought to get moving.

He straddled the bike and a flick of the wrist sent it out of the parking lot and down the road.

Traffic out of town was light, and soon the strip malls and the burger joints, the gas stations and the pawn shops faded away – the woman would be far behind him by evening; the money would keep her quiet. The city limit of Del Rio was marked by a green sign on the right side of the road as he left town. He took a left and continued west down Highway 90.

The water of Lake Amistad as he crossed the bridge was a royal blue reflection of the pale sky above it. The road was the same, black and infinite. The red shores were washed gently by the water, ebbing and flowing this side and that of the Mexican-American border. The shores and the water did not care whose they were, they only existed to erode one and to impede the other. Somewhere downriver there was a dam holding all that weight back. It was sure to one day crack and send a cascade of confusion crushing down on the territorial boundaries between Texas and Coahuila.

It isn't natural, that sort of thing.

An eagle soared and bent back on the updrafts above him. Its wings were hardly flapping at all; it just rode the breeze, its eyes leering downward at some unseen lizard in the gnarled, sparsely populated underbrush that pockmarked the face of the hard and barren earth on either side of the road with its quickly passing slashes of thin yellow line.

That road cut through the tops of ancient hills. On either side Jackson could hear the sound of the motor clack harshly off the walls. He could see the layers on layers of rock. The eons. The limestone where there was once sea. The red sandstone of an island that had poked its head above the shallow waters. Man can certainly mold the world as they so choose, Jackson thought. Instead of laying the road on top of these hills, they had blasted the centers out of them. The road was straight and flat.

The motor's echo clacked off the side walls of the once-hilltops when he rode through.

Another eagle soared on the updrafts of the wind above the road, this one tracking a snake that bathed in the noontime sun. The snake would slither off under the shelter of gnarled mesquite branches when it saw the eagle approach, and the eagle would lift itself once more on the updrafts to its perch on the wind.

The terrain to either side of the road was rocky and barren – the underlying features of the earth exposed like the skinned scalp of a man. Beneath this there was nothing but more rock until you reached the heat of the core that warmed the planet. The waving lines that radiated off of the asphalt distorted the faraway bends in the road, forming a confessional screen between Jackson and the horizon line.

By now, Hager had woken. He had seen that the truck had not returned, that the money was not on the kitchen table, that he had been had. He would have eaten breakfast – two eggs, over medium, two slices of toast, and a couple pieces of crispy fried bacon. He'd wash it down with orange juice when he finished. And then he would sit on the front porch, looking out over all of that golden field of hay that no cattle would be grazing, rocking in his chair.

He'd try to enjoy retirement for just one morning. The Thursday paper would give him some of the local news. He'd fold it and set it on the porch beside the rocking chair and look out over the field again, hoping to see a trail of dust billowing from his dirt driveway. But none was forthcoming. Only the occasional mockingbird or dove fluttered from the field.

Hager sat on that aged grey wooden porch and rocked in his chair, looking out at the golden fields of hay for a long time before his wife asked if he wanted her to phone the police. Hager nodded. The rocker creaked against the porch and its oiled wood was slick under Hager's hands as he worked his palms against the armrest. He'd made the chairs himself a few years back. He'd made the porch by hand many years before that. He'd driven every nail, and now the wood was warped and gnarled and dry, but it hadn't begun to rot. It was just old. And though the thing was old it still did its job. Maybe it creaked a little, maybe it wasn't the most visually appealing porch – the wood being grey, and there were knots that he hadn't bothered to take out scattered across the surface, but it held firm despite the rusty nails or the dry wood. His hair was grey too, and he had taken a few lumps on that head underneath it, but underneath that grey and those knots he still had a good brain. He was still a good man. Older, wiser.

He remembered the last days of the Old West. He remembered his grandfather telling him that if Hager was to be only one thing in his life that he'd better be honest. An honest man without a dime is worth more than all the dishonest men with all the money in all the banks in the world. Those men made the stock market crash back in '29, those men ruined honest men's lives. Those men took and took from honest men who worked their whole lives for a little spread of something and they never felt any heat from it at all. But not this time. Not this time.

If he couldn't make Jackson into a good man, couldn't make him into an honest one, then somebody else would have to set him straight.

"Sheriff'll be here shortly," his wife said, handing him a glass of tea.

Hager would force a small smile at her and take the glass and swirl the cubes of ice around in it. He would take a couple of sips and set the glass down on the grey wood of the porch. The cool condensation from the glass would soak into the pores of the grey wood porch and turn it brown.

The grey wood of dead trees flashed by Jackson's peripherals every so often. Some of them were the posts for tangled barbed-wire fences put up long ago when the highway was first laid to earth.

Another slash of yellow line and another eagle above.

The road bent left a while before straightening up. It cut through more prehistoric hilltops and there was the sound of the motor clacking violently against the wall like a skull being slammed against a metal workbench in some grotesque rendition of a metronome's steady tocking. Soundless clouds dotted the deep blue of the sky. It was silent a while, but the motor was singing. After a time, it becomes nothing more than background noise, that motor. You become accustomed to all the ticks and the vibrations. The whirring of the pistons hammering up and down is second nature to your ears. The hum of combustion becomes the new baseline by which you determine what silence really is. The road was silent, except when he rode through those gouges in the hilltops and heard the clacking.

Another. Then silence.

Then another.

Silence for longer now.

Then a clack. And another. Another still as the miles rolled by like the road and the motor were conspiring to tap out some message to him in Morse code.

And then another. This one was longer. There was the hollow clacking of the exhaust off of the limestone walls ringing in his ears, the tappets and valves ticking and ticking beneath him, and the layers of millions of years of limestone on the walls around him, built one on top of the other, stacked like a chimney. He could hear the sweet final note of the fishtails chirping gently at the end of each stroke of the motor, just before the echo off of the walls. Clack, tweet, clack, tweet, back and forth and so on to a beautiful crescendo as he twisted the throttle, and the tappets were tapping, and the flywheels that turned the motor whirring faster faster faster, and the chain in the primary and the chain on the rear wheel flying in an oblong snicksnicksnick-snick, and the wheels on the road with their tread that brushed the asphalt, and the wind that blew wildly through it all with its static white noise of the TV's bunny ears falling on the shag carpet of a living room, and the clacktweetclacktweet. And then nothing.

The road broke from the hilltop. The limestone walls whisked themselves away from his peripherals and were replaced with openness. And the clacking was gone, but the road noise was louder and there were steady thumps and a very faint echo – far away. He stood on the pegs of the Panhead. Perched up there he could see over the concrete railing of the bridge and down into the chasm some hundred feet below where the steel waters of the Pecos gently flowed – the walls high and sheer on either side, and the rocky banks no more than a couple of feet wide. Three goats drank at the edge of the river with their hooves gripping like sandpaper to the blank stone banks. In the air beside Jackson, small birds fluttered from one precipice to the other, twisting around each other back and forth like opposite strands of a double helix. The DNA of the

Earth – no smoky bowling alley or stuffy hotel room, just these birds fluttering in the wind with a backdrop of endless blue sky. South to north they frantically flapped their tiny wings to some other hideaway in the rock face. Off to the west the river bent gracefully like the final pose of a ballet recital, arm gesturing away around the corner and over that faraway horizon line where its waters met the Rio Grande and flowed to be mixed in the salty quagmire of the ocean.

He snapped his head back-and-forth vigorously, east to west, west to east. He smiled and dropped his rear to the low-slung seat of the motorcycle and gave a Whitmanesque yawp to the blue ceiling above him. Jackson lifted his left fist triumphantly into the air at a passing semi and heard the foggy bellowing of its horn behind him as he twisted hard on the throttle and was jerked backwards against the luggage by the Panhead's sudden change in momentum.

Jackson and the motorcycle zipped through the hallway of limestone on the other side of the bridge – hardly even noticing it, and roared into a wild blue open. The rocks and gnarled branches greeted him again as they baked in the afternoon sun. The motor was singing.

An opera, that's what they should write about him when it was all said and done. Something that captures the sound of the open road and the freedom of the Wild West, he thought. There was nothing like it. The sun on your face. The endless asphalt that your trusty steed would carry you down under that blue sky. The red dirt billowed on the plain.

He was a hero. A modern-day Buffalo Bill riding a watersmooth stallion. He was a handsome man. When he got to the next town, one smaller than Del Rio, he was sure he'd have to bat the ladies off with a stick. They'd want to feel the machine between their legs, maybe after that they'd feel him too. One two three four five, line 'em up from town to town, he thought. Desert women were desperate for a good-looking desperado. That's why they were out here, wasn't it? Fall in love with the striking stranger in a smoky pool hall and ride away into the sunset, then make love to him, then take his name once you found out he had a stake in Standard Oil; or felt the bundle of cash bulging in his pants when you undid his belt. Either way, Jackson had it made. He would be as legendary as any of the gunslingers of the old days.

❊ ❊ ❊

The next green sign on the side of the road read: Langtry 4 Sanderson 64.

Langtry.

The home of Judge Roy Bean: the last of the great men of the Old West; the last vestige of the Old West itself in fact.

The judge had led a life of antics and lawless majesty. As a young man he opened a trading post with his brother in Mexico, where he shot and killed a man. As a result, Roy Bean fled to San Diego, where his other brother was elected mayor in 1850. Political connections breed corruption. The handsome young Bean became the apple of the eyes of many young San Diegan ladies. Often, as many handsome young outlaws do, Bean found himself in trouble competing for the affection of women. He fought and won a duel against a man in winter of 1852, but was arrested and sent to prison on a charge of assault with intent to kill.

Bean spent months locked in the San Diego jail, but while he was there he received many gifts from the women in town. They would send him food, wine, fine cigars, cakes, clothes, and finally a set of knives that were cooked into the inside casings of a dozen tamales. Roy Bean then used these knives to dig through the cell wall of the jail and escape back into society in April of 1852. He hightailed it to another California town where his brother would later be murdered. Roy took over his saloon and carried on.

A few years later, Bean's latest love interest was kidnapped by Mexicans and forced to marry a wealthy officer. Bean, being the boisterous man that he was, tracked his woman and her captor down, claimed he could kill the officer in a duel, and did. After the death of their superior, the officer's men captured Bean and strung a noose around his neck. As Bean sat there on a horse, with the rope around his neck tied to a tree, the Mexican soldiers slapped at the horse's rear and egged it on to bolt and leave Bean swinging in the breeze. This went on for some time; still the horse would not budge, and eventually the Mexicans gave up and left Bean to die in the sun.

However, his rescued bride was hiding behind a pine nearby and cut the noose loose from the tree. She and Roy left California for New Mexico, where Roy Bean would run a saloon with "a fine billiard table" in Piños Altos with a rope burn around his neck for several years.

By 1861, the nation was at war. By March of the following year, the war had come to the New Mexico Territory. Hard fighting in the Glorieta Pass wound up a Union victory, and Roy Bean retreated from New Mexico with the Confederate forces. He spent twenty years in San Antonio, running supplies for the Confederate army, rustling cattle, and watering down milk he sold to people in town. These business ventures allowed him to marry, but when he headed for the West again, he left his woman and four children in San Antonio.

Men in the West are not family men. They drink and they fight and they bed prostitutes at night in wooden rooms lit by oil lamps. The black stains on the walls, the light of a cigarette when the lamps go out. These men rise and go about the day alone. They turn where they want, roll in the mud, and make decisions for the hell of it. They are all looking for gold. The prospectors, the saloon owners, the bank robbers, and the drunken barflies twist their necks and break their backs for all that glitters. And in this barren and harsh land where whiskey is easier to come by than a good drink of water, the gold does not come in rivers. Those looking are always looking. They may stop in at the watering hole from time to time, but their minds are always on the streams that bubble steadily. Then they find it, and they discover that sometimes the idea of a thing is often better than the thing itself, and so there must be something better over the next hill, the next town, another day's ride, because dreaming of Eldorado and setting up a residence there are two entirely different things. You arrive to great fanfare, but before long you begin to miss the silence of being anonymous. You leave without telling a soul and stop in nowhere on the way to where you are going. It is always over the next hill.

The next hill was Langtry, and Jackson Hunter rolled into that sleepy town on Highway 90 less than 100 years since Roy Bean decided that the Wild West tent-city at this location was the perfect place to reside. Now its streets were paved, the houses were of brick and board, telephone wires bisected the sky, the shoulders of the road were freshly mowed, and Jackson wondered when time began to move so fast.

He slowed the cycle to third gear, then to second. He turned into the town and the Harley putted slow and low on the empty street. The few houses on either side were dilapidated. There were cracks in the brick, the boards were rotted through, but there were cars parked out front of every one. Their paint shone in the afternoon sun. The longstanding Western tradition of having a fine horse whether or not you had a fine home had continued here through the postwar years. It was good to see that American excess always found a way.

Jackson pulled off the road into a dirt parking lot. He parked the motorcycle and stood by it for a while. There was the Jersey Lilly, just across the street. There were a few other cars in the parking lot – a Pontiac from Peach County, Georgia, two Ford F-100s, one from Indiana, the other from Missouri, and a beat up International with cracking blue paint and a cracked windshield from Alberta; none from Texas made the pilgrimage.

In the 1880's, it was different. Workers flocked to the railroads by the thousands looking for fast money, and Roy Bean exploited that just as he had everything else in his life. He set up a permanent residence in the tent-city that Langtry once was. Before long, Bean had practically named himself justice of the peace in the tiny town in the arid land west of the Pecos – promptly, in his first official act as the "Law West of the Pecos," he shot up the tent-saloon of a wealthy Jew in town, and then set up his own. The Jersey Lilly, as it came to be called, became the center of all the hubbub in the sixth precinct of Pecos County. The Honorable Judge Roy Bean set up his courtroom as an attachment to the saloon; from here he handed out his sentences, often siding with whichever lawyer spent more at the bar during recess from the proceedings. He laced the drinks with kerosene, he often bowed to the wills of men he found guilty – even going so far as to drop a hanging sentence from a particularly irate defendant. He ruled from the Revised Statutes of Texas, written in 1879, until damn near the turn of the century. Bean burned any newer books of law that ever made it to Langtry. He never erected a jail in the

47

town, so most punishments were handed out in the form of fines, which Bean pocketed. What else could he be expected to do? Riding to the county seat in Fort Stockton was out of the question, and the railroad only had a train come by every so often. Bean was a fair man. Where most were hung for stealing horses in other counties, Bean let them go if they promised to return the stolen livestock. All of them, every single one would hold his hat over his belt buckle, bow his head, and promise that he would do just that, and that he would never return to a life of crime.

Bean's popularity among horse-thieves, tres-passers, drunken lawyers, and bar-brawlers earned him re-election until the year 1896. Even in defeat, however, Bean could not be silenced. He refused to scrap his copy of the Revised Statutes of Texas or turn in his seal as Justice of the Peace.

After his time as Justice of the Peace in Pe-cos County officially ended, Bean became a legend in his own day. Heavyweights Bob Fitzsimmons and Peter Maher were two boxers at the top of the sport in 1896; the only problem was that boxing was out-lawed in both Texas and Mexico. Roy Bean had a solution.

Sitting on his back porch in Langtry, sipping a glass of kerosene-laced whiskey, Bean watched the Rio Grande River run slowly by. Roy could see the river rise and fall, and at a particular time of year, when it was at a certain depth, there was an island that formed in that aquatic border between Texas and Mexico. Bean made a few calls to friends and sent a few letters, and before he knew it Fitzsimmons and Maher, their entourages, the media, and rabid fans crowded the island. The bareknuckle brawl only lasted one minute and 35 seconds before Fitzsimmons was lifting the World Heavyweight Championship belt over his head. Bean was still on his back porch, sipping his whiskey.

Roy Bean died after a night of heavy drinking in 1903, sleeping peacefully in his own bed – a fate not many wild men of the West suffered. After his death the school wanted for free firewood in the wintertime, the poor wished Bean was there to give them a coat to wear or a meal to eat, and the rest of Roy Bean's once flourishing bank account was empty, given out to those who needed it more.

Not all good men are good men always, but the good is always in a man.

Jackson's eyes bored into their own reflection at the bar. He nursed a watered-down whiskey in the dimly-lit room. Those out-of-state cars in the parking lot all had drivers in the Jersey Lilly. They were little atomic families with painted-on smiles and flashing Polaroid cameras. They were drunken loners like him but with Canadian accents and a penchant for the word "eh" at the end of their sentences like some sort of maple-leafed punctuation. They were southern Black men on edge wondering if segregation had really ended this far out. They all milled about the museum and then to the bar as if they expected more than what it was. How little they made of the greatness of this gilded age past.

Roy Bean was a hero, Jackson thought as he sipped his next whiskey. He toasted to him loudly on his third, earning the cringing stares of the other tourists. And by the fourth he still could feel no effect. On the fifth glass he asked if it was even alcoholic whiskey. The sixth had him standing on the barstool slurring at the barkeep that his liquor was watered down, that he should be ashamed of himself for taking people's hard-earned money the way he was.

"It's all a fuckin sham!" he shouted as he exited the bar, and the barkeep slammed the door behind him.

The wind was blowing, kicking up dirt, dropping it someplace new.

❋ ❋ ❋

Jackson stood there for a while in the shade on the porch and watched the wind. It was invisible of course, but the dirt betrayed it. It gave away how the air moved, it danced in the sun, and swooped low in the shade, the wind twisted around gnarled trees, and tossed itself high into the air when it ran into the side of a building. Up there on the roof the wind-carried dirt would swirl back on itself like a wave when it breaks on a reef, twisting backwards and receding and destroying its own natural motion so much that by the time it reaches the shore – the opposite side of the building – it is nothing more than a quiet whimper of what it once was. It would slink off the edge where it lay in the shadows, waiting to be swept along by some other gust's power.

The world was gently swaying, and Jackson had looked at the wind for too long. The sun was beginning to fall in the western afternoon sky, and Sanderson was still a ways off. He wanted to be there before nightfall.

Jackson straddled the bike again and lifted the kickstand with his foot. He rested his right hand on the head of the motor, feeling for when that first sting from the aluminum would tell him that it was warmed up. He lifted his hand from the engine and rubbed his middle finger with his thumb where the bike had spoken to him. He gripped the throttle and revved it a couple of times. He heard the gargling roar and the tweet from the pipes. The lenses of his sunglasses were pockmarked with dead bugs, and the leather jacket he wore was unzipped.

The Panhead tore from the dirt parking lot and into the street, through the town, back to Highway 90, and away from Langtry and its civilization with the telephone wires, and the dilapidated houses with shining cars that kept the gas station in business, and the tourist hot-spot with the watered-down whiskey and the mirror behind the bottles of liquor row-on-row in that dimly-lit bar that reflected those hollow eyes holding nothing more than the rotting boards of a ceiling in them. The sky was still blue out there.

The road that stretched beneath it was smooth under Jackson's wheels. Though the thoughts always broke through, he tried to think of very little on that ride, only focusing on getting as far down the road and away from Uvalde as possible. The sheriff was surely at Hager's by now, and he'd be smoking a cigarette on their front porch, a yellow legal pad in his hand, a pen in the other – scribbling chicken scratch runes on the paper while he rattled off a series of questions to Hager and his wife.

"When's the last time you said you seen 'im?"

"Yesterday," Hager responded.

"'Bout 11:30," said his wife.

The sheriff looked over the top of his glasses. "How much money you said he had?"

"12,000 dollars in cash."

"Now Hager tell me why in the Sam Hill you'd've given that boy free reign over your money? Why wouldn't you go with 'im, knowing you got your entire livelihood ridin' on that line?"

Hager clenched his jaw and looked into his clasped hands in his lap.

"We trusted 'im," his wife said.

The sheriff looked over the top of his glasses at Mrs. Hager again and then back to Hager sitting in his old rocker. "Why the hell wouldn't you've taken a check?"

Hager looked up – defiant, "You think I trust the fuckin gubment knowin' anything to do with my money after what they let happen in '29? Was you even alive then, boy? And why the hell should I owe Uncle Sam another fuckin' penny in taxes after he whisked me away from my life here and told me I had to go kill Germans in the trenches in France? He ain't ask me shit and I don't owe him shit neither. You even understand what that's like Parker?

"Well no sir I don't. Some of us were volunteers."

"You were in the goddamn Navy, Parker, in the goddamn Atlantic. Why the hell am I settin' here getting grilled by some young sonofabitch sheriff who never seen a hard day in his dadgum life asking me the questions like it's my fault some other young shithead ran off with everything I ever worked for my whole fuckin' life?"

Hager's wife put her hands around his chest and he relaxed back into his rocker with his jaw clenched. "Now we just want some help, sheriff." She said, "Can you please help us? We'll give a reward."

Hager watched him drop his cigarette onto the wood of porch and crush it out with his boot. "Yes ma'am," Sheriff Parker said, "now why don't you tell me more about that vehicle you said he made off with?"

It was a once-white but now rusted 1958 Ford F-100. Jackson still knew the license plate number by heart. What he did not know was who the man he sold it to was, nor did he know where that man was headed, or if the sheriff would even care. Jackson had gotten on the most conspicuous vehicle he could've chosen, and that yellow Panhead had sent palms to the ears of more than one old woman in that gas station parking lot yesterday. If there was one thing you could be sure of, it's that a disrespected grandmother will always find her way of having revenge on you for what you did to her.

Uvalde was a small town. It wouldn't have taken the sheriff long to figure out where Jackson might have gone.

When the sheriff left the Hagers' he would head into town and stop off at the Texaco to fill up the cruiser. When he was there, he'd feel a little thirsty and go inside to grab a drink. When he paid for it, he'd ask the cashier how the day was going.

"Good, sir. How 'bout you?"

"Doin' alright. Say, you ain't happen to see that Hunter boy around here lately, have you? Fella that works down on ol' Hager's farm?"

"No I ain't seen 'im, but no wait, maybe I did. He ain't said nothing to me or acted too strange, but I did hear he stirred up some kinda ruckus in the parking lot the other day."

"What happened?"

"Well this ol' lady came in here all huffed up about something, tryin' to fix 'er hair, tossed her purse over 'er shoulder like she'dabout had it with somethin'. So I asked her if it was somethin' the matter. Next thing I know she's goin' on and on about how she always knew that ol' boy was trouble and she was gonna tell her granddaughter it was good that he ran off on her. Said he about started a brawl with two fellas on them chopper motorcycle lookin' things in the parkin' lot. Then the next thing she knows, ol' Jackson up and swaps keys with one of them fellas and goes rip roarin' out of here headed west on one of 'em – louder'n a gunshot. Lady said her 'ears was still ringin' when she was payin' for her Reds."

The sheriff would take down the man's name just in case he needed to get in touch with him again, he didn't tell the cashier what for, and then he would get in his squad car and head to the courthouse. He'd sit in his office with a pencil eraser pressed to his chin with an ankle thrown up on the opposite knee, and then he'd call the deputies and sheriffs from Uvalde to Del Rio, and the anthill of law enforcement would burst open.

They'd find sweet morsels on the route Jackson had taken and bring them back to the den unless he could put enough distance between himself and the paper trail. It was good that he was in a desert. Those long distances between towns would do nothing but serve him now.

Until they catch you. But they aren't going to catch me, he thought. Yes they are. You know they will catch you just like they caught all of those outlaws before you. Do you think you are special? Do you think you can really get away? You will not. They have brought down better men than you, those real outlaws in the old days. You are nothing but a cheap imitation, an aftermarket replacement part; you are not those men you admire. How could you be? You are a coward. I am not a coward, he thought. You are a coward and you will always be a coward. No. Then how did you end up here? Do you think that these roads just bend for you? You ran along them. You bolted without speaking to a soul, there was no conflict, no struggle; you did nothing to earn what you now have. You are a coward, and you have come into your station in life by virtue of being a coward – this much is certain. You are not a good man. You are not brave. You will cower when they corner you behind a motorcycle that will not help you run and will not conceal you from the photographers nor shield you from the lead that those guns fire. You will die a coward's death as cowards deserve to die, so huddle for warmth, enjoy the sun while it is on your face, soon it will be replaced by dirt, though you deserve the bottom of a river – and even there, with all that over your eyes to shield you from the painful reality of the truth, you would turn your eyes down and cower. Yet you stare into boards; why can you not face it!

※ ※ ※

The wind was a nuisance now. It tore at his sleeves and pressed him firmly against the luggage behind him. His arms and back and neck were sore from resisting it. His face was raw from the wind, and his eyes were dried out – the insides of his eyelids felt like a cat's tongue against his cornea each time he blinked. The unseasonably warm January sun was overhead, and the Panhead felt every bump and jitter in the asphalt beneath.

The little mechanical birds were still singing beneath Jackson, but there was something off in the symphony. Just one missing note, some flutist that was a line behind, or a drummer who had lost a stick, now playing with one. It began small, but soon the imperfection affected the whole sound of the machine – the whole woodwind section was gone, the percussionists had let their symbols clatter to the floor, and the tubas' whomp of vibratory noise swept through the whole ensemble, deadening the space. The gas tank clattered against the frame. The motor beneath it was struggling now, a piston would fire, but the next would not, and gas would overload in the combustion chamber and backfire out the fish-tail exhaust brackishly. The sound of it was like drinking water tainted with salt.

Jackson looked between his knees and twisted on the throttle. The bike jetted forward and then lugged down, and it happened again as he twisted another time. And now the percussionists had set to tossing their kits around the stage. The brass was all dented, and the guitars were slamming against the ground until the sound of the motor was dead and there was nothing but the whining feed-back of empty noise and the tires spinning on their axles until the Harley came to a whimpering halt a quarter mile down the road.

The wind was there still, cutting from south to north across the plain, and Jackson stood with his hands on his hips at the edge of the road, staring at the bike. He tried to start it. He twisted the throttle twice and kicked through slow on the kicker pedal. Then once more. He turned the key on and felt the compression of the motor build on his foot. The quiet clicks of the ratcheting kicker pedal. Jackson lifted himself up into the air on the top of the pedal and brought himself swinging down along its pendulum. The bike should've snapped to life. It should have fired and roared out across the desert to whatever walls the noise would echo off of that it was alive. There was silence. There was the heat of the sun.

It was running a moment ago, and now it was not; that was the only thing he could be sure of. Beyond it, he was at a loss. There is nothing so alien as unfamiliar machinery. He could try to dismantle the Harley. Maybe he would discover some defective part, some broken bolt that had snapped off at 60 miles an hour and caused the motorcycle to sputter and pop and then go still, but Jackson didn't know where he would begin. The nuts and bolts of the thing were a mystery, to take the bike apart to try and figure out what was wrong and then put it back together would have been like scrambling a perfectly arranged Rubik's Cube.

He looked up the road, both the asphalt that way and the direction he came were empty except for the wavering lines of heat radiating up from the surface. Jackson tried to remember how many cars he had seen on the road here. Not many. There were the few in the parking lot of the Jersey Lilly, a couple of semis – maybe – since he had left Del Rio. There was only fence strung up on rotted and dried limbs of long-dead trees from some place other than here. The only vegetation that grew were the ankle-high shrubs and the cactus and the odd patch of grass that would sprout whenever the rains came. They would not be coming today, the few clouds of earlier had fled the sky and now it was an empty open blue that met red on all 360 degrees of horizon.

"Shit."

Jackson sat down in the dirt on the shaded side of the motorcycle and watched a bird wing its way to the east. He clacked pebbles together in his hand for a while, and then he whittled an impossibly small twig down to nothing, and still no cars had come along the highway.

But what about when they did? He thought. They are going to spot you; you're impossible to miss sitting here, and yes, that car could be a good-Samaritan-well-to-do stranger who will help you out and load this old machine that you know nothing about into the bed of their truck, but the car could also have sirens and flashing lights, and they will drag you to jail where you will have no money and no freedom and no sky in 360 degrees all around you, and in that jail you will sit and stare at the ceiling like you always do, not thinking, not moving, just sitting and staring and noticing those tiny imperfections in the boards that no man should care for enough to take note of, and you will beg again for the transfixion of the dust in the wind or the oiled lanes of the bowling alley or the rancid taste of the tomato and wish to whatever god you have that you had not been such a coward and that you had fought when they spotted you, but you will never fight. You are a coward. So now, in this moment, the best thing to do is to be the coward that you are. Run and hide through the night, and maybe in the morning you will have an idea or a stroke of luck to guide you next.

Jackson stood. He pulled the kickstand up with his foot and began to push the bike down the road. It was hot, and he began to sweat in the afternoon sun, so he hung his jacket on the sissy bar, and there it tousled in the breeze. After a while he crested a small hill, and on the other side the pushing was easier. Then it was hard again when the road flattened out. A man must do the difficult things, but a horse needs no pushing.

The breeze stopped, and the sun was low, and the sky was red again. Off to the right there was a rickety old tin gate and a narrow dirt path that wound through the desert to some place where a man was still hoping for the rains to come. He surely wouldn't mind. The gate shuddered and shook when Jackson pushed it open. The dirt of the path shifted beneath his feet and had its own ideas about where the Harley's wheels would be going. They found every crevice and stone in that sand, and the bike nearly fell over twice, but Jackson was able to keep her steady. The going was slow, and the sky was purple, and a half mile of pushing down that road led Jackson to a rocky outcropping of stone that had once been lava that would serve to shield him from the winds that were now picking up again.

He wasn't the first to seek shelter here. There were a few sticks stacked near a pit of ash and some logs that must have been brought in from a store in Del Rio. Jackson leaned the bike on its kick-stand and climbed to the top of the rocks. He watched the sun setting in the west and felt the pale presence of the nearly full moon rising behind him in the east – its translucent glow mixing with the melting mishmash of color in those thin clouds on that faraway western horizon. The sun dipped below the line and took the red and the orange with it. The yellow and purple were soon to follow, slowly drip-ping beyond the point of no return like an hourglass, until the sky was dark except for the moon, and the wind came rushing back to him. He'd left his jacket dangling from the sissy bar of the Panhead, and the breeze on his sweaty shirt made him cold. But he stayed up there a while looking west across the high-way where still no cars had driven by.

Eventually some had to. Where were the tourists from Langtry? Where were the long-haul truckers and the red-eyed ranch hands making their way home at the end of the day or to the nearest bar or delivering livestock to a customer? They aren't trusted for that anymore.

The clouds were all smearing the horizon. It was as though he was in a bubble of clear air and surrounded by a ring of nebulosity. Far off in the distance to the south, beyond the horizon line, he could see the bright orange of Del Rio reflecting off the bottom of the clouds. They stood out as the only color in the pale-swept surroundings under the light of the moon. Their underbellies softly burbling with fluorescent hues that even out here were impossible to escape. And that glowing mass over there signaled to the heavens where the town was, as if it were defiantly shoving a middle finger in the face of a man shouting for it to get off his lawn – like a dot on a paper map. And he realized how lonely he was, and how big this world is. It is such a long way from home out here. His only companions were the motorcycle and those softly-lit orange underbellies of once colorless cloud, but all of those lights were shining down. They were not for him. They were for those milling crowds of mindless clones naively pretending that the night and its darkness and uncertainty did not exist, and for the police who were hot on his trail leaving the motel where he'd stayed the night before – on the hunt for a man on the run. The machine was quiet and lifeless behind him, and Jackson was alone again.

The moon was shining bright when Jackson descended the rocks, and it made every stone cast sharp shadows against the ground, and he could see for miles around him, and there was the silence and the cool air. He put on his jacket and took the pack off the sissy bar of the motorcycle. He rolled out a sleeping bag and found a Zippo lighter and some fuel for it. There were some army rations and a mess kit, a flask of whiskey, a pair of socks, a towel, and a tool roll filled with wrenches and screwdrivers that were rusty and grimy, an owner's manual for the Harley-Davidson Panhead: 1948-1957. He tossed most of it to the side.

The young man stacked the twigs neatly in the ash pit, then soaked one of the socks in the lighter fluid and used it to start the fire. It lit with a whoosh, sucking the air powerfully from above itself and then subsided to a gentle crackle that occasionally threw a spark or two into the wind that streamlined from over the top of the rocks.

Jackson leaned with his back against them and looked at his motorcycle while he ate the rations. They weren't good, but they had enough tack to them to be edible.

"What the hell am I going to do?" he asked to the motorcycle and the crackle and pop from the fire. The motorcycle was silent still, and the crackles and pops of the fire did not break their rhythm; the flames just danced and the moon watched it all from high above, hanging there like a prop in a stage production. Its light baked the whole desert into two dimensions. The shrubs and rocks and the cacti before him looked like they were all cardboard cutouts stapled flat to a wall. The horizon seemed an inch away from his nose.

There was nothing but the fire and the man and the sleeping bag rolled out next to the motorcycle on the leeward side of a prehistoric outcropping of rock. Sometimes you are alone. But where were the vaqueros and the vagabonds and the vigilantes? The characters that came out of the woodwork and drew to the fire like moths, and they cooked steaks over the open flame and told stories and sang songs and plucked guitars and wrapped their serapes tightly around their shoulders. They were all in yesterday. They were all stuck in a time from when the starlight came. They were trapped in their carvings on the rocks. 1871. 1903. 1962. 1912. 1899. 1900.

1947. 1968. 1886. The glyphs of strange beings playing the flute from a time before that. Jackson scratched his own year next to those. Your life seems like a long time until you remember that everyone else's has seemed that way too. The firelight danced and flickered off the blade as he dulled the point of his knife on the stone, and the dust fell in tiny fragments like snowflakes.

The moon was high above now, and the only shadows that were cast were done so from the light of the fire, and they were long and their edges ephemeral, and they seemed to stretch all the way to the horizon – beyond that, surely into space. That sickening distance began to overwhelm him. Trying to factor the time was no help – those who had tried to navigate it all wound up buried beneath the same earth. He lamented. Speaking to the heavens was no good either. All that light from those stars so long ago only matters to us now. What once was guides what is – the astrolabe, the compass, the sail, and the sun. There is no way into yesterday. But what you carve into the stone is known only to you.

What were they before time? Before the clocks, and the calendars, and the songs, and the almanacs, and the watches, and the lights automatically metered to turn on when the sun was gone and off when it came back, what existed? The meter of the world was written in the heavens, and the sun came and went and denoted to you when the next day began and when the previous had ended. The stars circled around Polaris, the constellations waged war and lived out the same lives trip after trip around the sun. Was watching that same story play out over and over again above him how man determined what he was supposed to do? Before they were American, or Texan, or Canadian, or bartender, or psychiatrist, or lonely man in his small apartment overlooking downtown Paris with all its lights and illuminated streets, before men and women who wandered those alleys looking for someone to serve them what they desired in exchange for those bills that he let softly drop one by one into the flames of the fire, what were they?

Maybe they were mankind.

A single tribe living under the great heavens, unspoiled by the modern way. Did they have hopes and dreams? Reality and fantasy? Love and hate?

They existed and went on; when they were done with that, they went to the same ground that we all return to. Was every day the same? A man discovered fire. An everyday struggle for survival requires man to change it up. Exploit the same resource day after day, year after year, and it will dry up – you will starve after you watch your children slowly wither away. Something must always be changing for man to thrive as man should.

But that is not what you are here for. This you know. This you have learned. Here is the question: Are good men a necessary evil, or have we constrained ourselves to a simple way of being that does not allow for change caused by wild men like you? Eve. Cain. Alexander. Caesar. Brutus. The Lionheart. Joan of Arc. Washington. Calamity Jane. These names you know. These are not good men, but they have been martyrized for what they did, and the word – say it – hero – follows closely on the lips of all who speak truly of them and with goodness in their heart. Those men destroyed the worlds of others for the good of their own. Good men are the downfall of the world. They keep the order in check – day after day, year after year they beat those down who would oppose them. Keep the wheel turning. Sustain the status quo so that society endures. Society stifles. Man desires change, a constant upheaval of what is moral and what is good. Look back at all you know and begin to understand that in history the only things you comprehend are moments of immense change – the rest is all filler for that dull void that is the livelihood of man. Stop the wheel. All that is mundane is *inhuman*, put there by those who wish to eliminate what makes us man. Take the knife, plunge it into those who rule and you become the ruler and the one who seizes destiny – history. This world will swallow you whole without a single care. She will cast you to the same loamy destiny that awaits all men if you let her. Some pervade. Some exist far beyond their time, and virtually all those who do, do so because they have altered the wheel, not simply hitched a ride. They cease to become man or woman and become we – a part of our story – we – humanity – mankind. You know what they are – say it – "hero."

And the flames danced at his back, and the whiskey flask was empty. The inside of the sleeping bag was safe and warm, and his leather jacket was rolled up beneath his head, and sleep did not come all at once to him, but it came as the surface of a ship in a storm – the swaying, then a dip and a splash of that cold darkness, and the rocks were bathed in the firelight – a wave that lifts you up high, then the weightlessness, and the heavy pulsating of the characters carved into the rocks – then the trough, and the shuddering of the planks, and the cascading of icy water that snatches the breath from your lungs, and the wave crashing over the bow, and the warmth of the fire, the weight of it all pulling you ever down, and a surrender to darkness.

The snapping open of your eyes in the weightless body to see the sky has come alive. The billions of pinpoints in the dark ceiling of the world are pushing you down, stifling you. They possess the power of a billion billion worlds from endless eons, and they form together in bright and milky masses murked by nebulas – a scar – a shattering in the mirror of Earth. The scar and the stars within bear upon you and you feel their weight push you back into your place. There in that sleeping bag. They are the only constants – the stars and the eyes. The embers of the fire. The warmth. And you surrender again.

And your eyes open and see that dawn is not far off. They only last so long.

It is as though you only blinked and the sky is on fire. And every cloud bears its own unique color as if the sun too is showing you that power of the cosmos. More shades of orange and red and purple than there are stars in the sky. You look at them a while and the remnant of the fire is softly sending spindles of smoke into the air to join them. It is still warm.

A quick flash of darkness.

And your eyes are greeted with that simple shade of blue. That kind of blue that follows you wherever you go, tugging at your back pocket, reminding you that you will always have it, reminding you that you are where you belong.

✳ ✳ ✳

He rose from the sleeping bag a worldly man. He brushed the ash from the top of the coals and blew on them until they were glowing orange. The land was no longer whitewashed, and the rocks behind him were red again; the Harley leaned lifeless on its kickstand.

74

Jackson climbed again to the top of the rocks. The road was empty as before. In the cloudless light of the day he could not make out where he had come from by the lights shining in Del Rio. It was an empty and new place – the same as before – populated only by the shrubs and whatever animals scurried beneath them.

The package of army rations opened with a tug at the corner, and Jackson ate.

He kicked dirt over the ashes of the fire and the few corners of unburned bills and adjusted his leather jacket on his shoulders. He made sure what was left of the money was still bundled in his back pocket, and he kicked the kickstand up against the frame of the motorcycle and began pushing it through the sand.

As before, the tires were impossible to keep straight on the dirt path. The sand was constantly shifting beneath their treads and Jackson cut a winding path down that already winding road. The going was slow. He hit a rock here, a divot in the road there. The bike was begging to lay on its side and rest, but machine and man trudged on.

He was rounding the final bend of the path when he heard the sound of tires on the highway. He bolted with the motorcycle, breaking into a full-out sprint through the sand towards the road. There were the flashing bulbs of the police car. It was rolling slowly along Highway 90. The cop inside had his transmitter in hand, and his sunglass-screened eyes scanned either direction, gazing out over the shrubs. He was looking west. Jackson saw him first; his hands tightened on the handlebars of the motorcycle, and he pulled hard on it as he threw himself to the ground, toppling the bike over on its side in the dirt and crushing his own leg.

He lay there biting down hard on his lip until he could no longer hear the sound of the rolling tires. He kicked himself free of the weight of the Harley and pressed his hand down firmly on the growing pool of red on his pant leg.

"Look what you've done," he said to himself. His jaw tightened. "Oh, it fucking hurts. Oh fuck."

He undid his belt and pulled off his pants. Just above the knee, the laceration was deep and oozing the warmth of the blood. The breeze on it stung like the needle of a wasp. "Holy fuck," he said.

76

He plopped his back on the ground and bit into a clenched fist red with blood and stifled the scream somewhere within his throat, and the blue sky was above him; only now there were white puffy clouds rolling in from the northeast, and the plain was flat, and the dark spots and the dizziness were morphing the landscape into something else.

"No," Jackson said. "No, no no, nononononono." He clinched his whole body and writhed on the ground and held it together. He could feel the lump of cash in his back pocket pressing itself flat between his weight and the desert floor. He stood. He hobbled on the one leg and somehow willed the bike upright. The black spots were coming again. The peripherals of his vision began to close in around the top of the Harley's gas tank. The yellow paint. Encompassing more and more of the total of his vision like the growing whistle of an oncoming train.

※ ※ ※

"Heavens above, my friend. What have you done to yourself?"

A man was standing over him, blocking out the view of the slow-moving white clouds in the sky. The sun was high overhead now. Jackson heard a vehicle idling. He saw the man again and reached clumsily and viscously for his belt.

"No, my friend. I am only here for to help you."

Jackson had unsheathed the knife, but let it fall into the dirt. The man with the dirty pants and spectacled face and impossibly clean fingernails reached for it, and Jackson let him take the blade.

"I will be back," the man said.

He heard his footsteps go towards the sound of the idling car, and he saw the clouds lumbering through the blue sky above. The motorcycle was upright beside him – standing guard. He heard the sound of rushing, concentrated air from the direction of the idling car. Like a propane torch would make, he thought. What is propane? To-orch. The way the teeth touch but don't touch when you say the word. The clouds are there but I am here. So I did not get lucky. Remember the slot machine? Pull the lever. Hear the whir. The clinking of the coins when they fell in the slot. On a boat. The kind with the wheel on the side. On the river. No, not the river. Not the river. Not the river, not the river. It wasn't that river. Something is within you. Like an ice cube, but not an ice cube. It is growing. Oh my, is it ever growing. A sizzling. Open your eyes!

His eyes electrified and he bolted upright. The veins on his neck stood out and his head convulsed back and forth. The scream stifled in his throat, and the man knelt holding the red-hot blade of the knife firmly down upon his thigh – his other hand clenching the leg higher up, and his eyes darting back and forth between the veins on Jackson's neck and the sizzling, popping of the blood pooling from the wound until the pain in Jackson was gone and he felt only a warmth in his lower extremities. He lay on his back. His eyes were wide and empty, and he heard the hiss of the knife each time it was reapplied.

The spilling of the blood was gone, replaced now only by the tightness of cauterized skin and the heavy aroma of burnt flesh. Jackson groaned as the man wheeled the motorcycle away, but the man paid him no attention. Jackson rolled on his side to see the man pull the tailgate of the truck down. He pulled a two-by-twelve from the bed of the Chevy to make a ramp to the ground. His white hair shone in the sun. He pulled the motorcycle around and lined it up with the board and pushed it into the bed of the truck without a hitch like a well-practiced equestrian might parade a horse. He tied the bike down and closed the tailgate. He walked to Jackson and offered him a hand.

"Can you stand?"

Jackson looked himself over. He thought he could, and with the help of the old man he stood upright and limped to the truck and got in.

They drove without speaking. The radio signal came and went. It was static and rolling wheels the whole way to Sanderson.

"I am going to drop you off here," the old man said as he pulled over to the shoulder of the road in front of the Eagle's Nest Café. "I will be back." Jackson climbed out and shut the door. He stood lightly on his left leg and looked down the road in either direction. There was a bend away to the south in the direction he had come, and high red rocks with sheer cliff faces jutted into the sky. Off to the west the road booked a straight ticket out of the tiny town, passing another high rock formation with steep sides on its way. The road was empty, a bird circled overhead in the early afternoon sun. Jackson wondered about the old man, but decided he could trust him. He'd brought him all this way, after all.

The name of the café was painted on the front windows, and inside he could see tables full of people. He wondered where they came from. Jackson walked through the door and found a seat at the bar.

"I'll be right with you in a minute now honey," a waitress in a blue apron said to him.

Jackson nodded and looked down at the menu and held a hand tight to his throbbing leg.

Every table in the café was full. Must be the lunch rush, he thought. The waitress made her rounds through the café. She had casual conversation with all of the old men – she asked about their wives. She chatted up the ladies out for lunch together, and laughed at a joke the gas station attendant from across the street told her when he paid his bill.

"What're you havin'?" she asked.

"Just a coffee, please."

"Just a coffee? We got pancakes, egg sand-wiches, chicken fried steak. Whatever you want."

"Just a coffee, please," he said.

"Well alright. Gimme a holler if you change yer mind."

She made her rounds through the café as more folks from the town came in and sat at the ta-bles. She seemed to know them all. Jackson nursed his coffee and tried to keep his mind off of the pain in his leg. It wasn't so much a throb as an ache now. Why is pain so difficult to ignore if you are not trying to save your own life through it? It fries the brain like electric shocks. It makes your thoughts scat-tered and random unless you are thinking about solely the pain itself – where it came from – how the pain is seeping through your body, and you cannot focus on trying to think of the desert or the wind or that bird circling high overhead to the mountain-tops, nor can you imagine the stars or the sunrise that you saw this morning. It is only the pain. Let it envelop you. Let it consume you as it does to men.

His forehead was leaning against the rim of his coffee cup. His teeth were gritting together in that chalky motion. His good leg bounced up and down vigorously, and the bad one hung limp from the barstool. The people behind him were all talking about the football team or the railroad or the vanishing jobs or the weather, and their voices echoed against the inside of those windows painted with the name of the café – the Eagle's Nest. The bird flying over the mountaintop. The sky. Think of the sky.

"Why the long face?" the waitress asked.

Jackson looked up at her. She was beautiful, and she had some kind of stain on the collar of her otherwise perfectly white shirt beneath the blue apron. She wore stud earrings. They were gold. The color of the motorcycle almost. Yesterday had been a better day. "Took a little spill this morning," he said. "Cut m'self up pretty good."

"You need some aspirin?" she asked. Before he could tell her no thanks she had dug into the pocket of her apron and dropped three pills onto the counter in front of Jackson's coffee cup. "I'm gonna put you in for a order of blueberry pancakes too." She furrowed her brow in concern at the tear in Jackson's jeans as she walked to take an order from the man who'd just sat down.

Jackson took the pills and swallowed them all without taking a sip of his coffee. They were uncomfortable on the way down.

The waitress took the man's order and came back to give Jackson his plate. He ate the pancakes slowly and sipped his coffee. He asked for another.

"So what brings you here?" the waitress asked as she poured the drink.

"Not sure."

"Not sure? People don't just up and run off to Sanderson, Texas on a whim, honey."

"You ever woke up one morning and realized the life that you were living wasn't the one that you wanted to live?"

The waitress grinned at Jackson. She set the coffee pot back on the warmer and went around to all of the tables. She laughed with the customers and said hello to old friends that she had seen every day for a very long time. She came back past the counter with arms laden heavily with dirty plates and half-eaten food. She set them down for the dishwasher to take and clean and turned back to Jackson with her hands on her hips and a stray hair falling over her forehead. "Every day of my fucking life," she said.

Jackson smiled and took another bite of the pancakes.

"What's your name?" she asked, "I'm Cindy."

"Nice to meet you, Cindy."

"You don't have a name, honey?"

"None to speak of. You can keep calling me that if you like."

Cindy shook her head and rolled her eyes, "You ain't my honey, honey."

Jackson smiled. He finished the pancakes and looked after Cindy as she made her rounds through the café again. It was a nice place. The floors were clean, and the aquamarine tables had chrome accents. It felt like the kind of diner his parents might have met at. They had been gone so very long. They might've ordered a malt together, they could have shared it and went for a walk down the street to the movie theater, but there was none in Sanderson. The closest was probably in Del Rio. Jackson wondered if they showed westerns in the West. They couldn't hardly be called westerns when you lived western, could they? Maybe he should ask

Cindy. You should ask no one anything. Do not forget what you are running from. But forgetting is the only thing to do. What else is there? I am here now. A strange man has helped me from somewhere in the desert to this tiny town. The man has taken the motorcycle somewhere; he may never be seen again. And if the police come there will be no way of running on only one leg. There is nowhere to hide here and I have doomed myself by stopping at the only two business establishments since Del Rio. The maid will talk, and if the police can understand what she says then they will be headed in the right direction. They are probably milling all about these parts. You have seen them; you have hidden from them so far. You betray yourself; you give up now to eat blueberry pancakes and live out some notion that every woman in the West dreams of a "desperado" like you to come through town. That is all there are out here; you are nothing special. Where is the fight you showed with the woman? Where is the desperation of the true desperado you had in you when you hid earlier this morning? You bear the scars. Honor them. But that was when there was a choice in the matter. Now there is nothing. It is all up to fate. Fate! Fate is for the stars, and you are but a man. A man can always alter his fate. The power of the cosmos is in everything. That is the destiny of man – that is the power of the cosmos in man. A man can always wake one morning and start anew. If a man does not like where his life is headed, he can turn right around and start in a new direction all over again. That's the beauty of it. That's what makes it worthwhile. Your life is nothing but emptiness until you try to alter your own fate. Your life is rotting boards without action. Do you think a rotting board can change fate? A rotting board blocks out the stars. Rotting boards control fate whether you want it or not. Coffins. Ceilings. *Gunsmoke.* Pick up. Tear them down. Start anew once more. Your life is stagnant if you allow it to be. And stagnating here over a plate of blueberry pancakes will only bring about the kind of out-of-your-hands fate-altering change that you wish to never go through again. Yet here you are, still going through it in your cowardice. You know it is true. Hager knows as well. You fought no one, you robbed no one; you are a petty thief and a criminal with the false notion that he is honorable. You are not an outlaw; you are a *coward.* But I am a man. And a man has the power to change his fate if he so chooses. So when they come for me I will choose the new fate, but for now, I will enjoy these final moments of the course that I am running. When the time comes I will fight, and there will be another course to be run. Until there is not. All courses come to an end. Some – your heroes – are worth telling of. But yours, yours will not be. You are not the great hero; you are not the great changer of worlds. You are Jackson Hunter. And I have changed my course before and I will do it again. I have chosen these paths and harmed these people, and I am not a good man, but I have these final moments to enjoy what there is. Sometimes that is all a man has. And these people do not yet know what I am, but they will. And when they know we will find a new way, and they will sing an opera for me and I will be a new incarnation of all that is good in the Old West. This is how men live their lives. You have chosen a path already marked, and yet you have deviated at every convenient turn. You are not a great man. You only follow the course. Yes, you have taken this money and mounted this steed, but since, you have taken the path of least resistance at every split in the trail. You follow. You are a canoe without an oar in the stream. Your heroes have sails. They mold the world into what they require it to be.

And do I not?

The café was empty and the front door opened, letting in a warm draught of air. The old man stood in the breeze, "Come," he said to Jackson Hunter.

Jackson stood and limped out the door.

"In the bed," the old man told him.

The motorcycle was gone, and Jackson somehow slung himself over the bedrails of the truck. Soon the old man came out of the café with Cindy behind him. "Guess you're comin' home for supper?" she asked.

"Well I guess so."

The pair got in the cab of the pickup and the truck pulled off down the road.

They turned right just outside of town. Cindy got out of the truck and unchained the gate. They pulled through and she got back in the pickup without closing it again. The road they were on was much the same as the one Jackson had camped down the night before – it was windy and shifted beneath the wheels of the truck as they drove up the gradual slope of the backside of one of the mountains Jackson had seen from the front door of The Eagle's Nest. They crested the slope of the mountain and drove along a steep bluff that looked off over the valley to the west.

The sun was setting again. The sky was orange. Far below, Jackson could see the black line of Highway 90 unfurling to the point where the ground met the sky. A semi was headed towards Sanderson, and a small car turned west onto the highway off of a dirt road.

The bumps of the driveway jarred Jackson in the bed, but the ache in his leg was mostly gone now. The hot knife had cauterized the wound and deadened the nerves. Now came the stiffness. He could hear the rocks being strewn about by the tires of the truck, and up ahead a chicken cawed at the sudden change in his world as the truck pulled up to the little clay-colored adobe house that was the old man and Cindy's home.

There were roosters pecking at the ground in front of the house. Around the side there was a chicken coop where soft coos of hens on their eggs could be heard. To Jackson's left there was a separate garage with the door open and the lights on inside. Through the door he could see the yellow Panhead sitting under the fluorescent glow.

He scooted out of the bed of the truck and hobbled to Cindy and the old man on the front porch and sat down in a wicker rocking chair.

"I'll go ahead and get supper started, Cindy said, "I s'pose you two'll be workin' on that bike out there."

"There is not much work to be done to the Harley-Davidson." The old man winked at Cindy, "Maybe only to the rider."

"Well that's even better. You'll be able to help with supper."

"Come along my friend. We have much work to be done."

Jackson was sitting in the wicker rocker with his bad leg stretched out before him. "Can't it wait a minute? The legs feelin' stiffer'n hell."

"No," the old man said, a hint of agitation in his voice, "it cannot wait for a minute. You will be fine to walk over to the garage and sit on a stool and do that what must be done." He grabbed Jackson by the arm and pulled him to his feet. "A little pain has never made weaker the man. A man must face a little suffering; how else will he know to enjoy the pleasant times?"

He let Jackson lean on him as they walked to the garage. Inside, everything was neatly organized. It was clear that every tool had a specific spot in the garage. The posters and old faded photographs of motorcycles that lined the walls were all hung sharply and level with one another. There was a motorcycle lift near the back of the twenty-by-twenty room, but the Panhead was sitting on the concrete floor. The old man sat in a recliner near the window and gestured to a low stool for Jackson to sit in. He sat and looked at the old man, who said nothing. He only opened his palms toward the bike as if to say, "There it is."

"What's wrong with it?" Jackson asked.

"Ah, yes. The age-old question."

Jackson looked at the old man. He looked as though he had nothing more to say. His palms were still open towards the bike. His eyes were bright behind the lenses of the glasses.

"I don't know what that means."

92

"So you are saying you do not know where to begin?"

"I don't know nothin' about this thing."

"That, my friend, is a lie. Otherwise you would not have made it as far as you did to pass out on my ranch."

Jackson looked down at the floor.

"No, do not be ashamed, my friend, I am not upset with you. I only wish for you to fix your problem with the Panhead."

"I told you I don't know nothin' about this thing."

"You must know *something*. A man cannot travel with his machine if he knows nothing about it. It would be like writing the Constitution if one did not know English. You must learn of the thing, or it will never help you. Otherwise it is all senseless gibberish. I can assure you that there is no machine ever designed as such." He gestured to the pictures on the walls. "Now, tell me what you know."

"It's yellow."

The old man stifled a smile. "Yes, now we are getting somewhere. More! Tell me what you know."

Jackson stared at the motorcycle for a while. It was all gibberish to him. There were nuts and bolts that held the thing together, but he didn't have the first clue how it all worked. He knew when he twisted the throttle it went fast, and when he pressed the brakes it slowed down. Somehow when he held in the clutch and lifted his left foot the thing would change gears inside the transmission, but none of it made any sense. "I don't know," he said.

The old man sighed. "Well, if you do not know more, then nothing can be helped. Certainly you must know something, otherwise I will have to tow you back down to the town and you can get yourself a motel room."

Jackson stared at the bike again – a mass of fastened nuts and bolts and steel and chrome. It had a headlight, a very long front end with a large wheel at the end of it. There were springs on the front end closest the headlight. Behind that there was the yellow gas tank with the cracking old paint. Beneath that was the Panhead engine. Its flat surfaces were shiny. He knew that inside of that dress the motor worked when he went down the road. There was the dome of the carburetor stuck to the side of the motor – tubes and wires ran from it to the gas tank and the throttle on the rabbit-ear handlebars that curled back over the yellow gas tank. The frame of the Harley was painted yellow too. It had a low-slung black leather seat that could hold both the rider, slightly above and behind the engine, and a passenger over the rear fender. In place of the passenger was the army duffel bag that held all of the supplies in it. Beneath the duffel bag was the transmission – the kicker arm protruded out and up vertically from it and the kicker pedal of yellow rubber hung like a trapezoid facing the engine. Behind the transmission was the rear tire and its spokes of chrome. From either side of the axle of the rear tire, two three-foot-long tubes of steel shot upwards into the sky and connected over the center of the rear fender, forming the sissy bar. Beside the sissy bar were two fishtail exhaust pipes that stretched from both the pan-shaped heads of the engine. They were what made the motor sing when he was flying down the road.

"I know it sounds like birds singin' when I'm goin'."

"Good," the old man said. "So you know something, and you really ride the thing, but think before you are going down the road. Picture her sitting in the parking lot. Picture her at the gas pump. What do you know then?"

"How I need to start it."

"Yes. Show me."

Jackson stood from the little stool and put his hand on the throttle of the bike.

"Think about what you are doing as you do it."

He twisted the grip of the throttle once, and then a second time. He turned the pedal of the kicker outward and pressed down on it until it swung through the bottom, and then he heard the clicks and felt the spring-like tension build up on the pedal as he kicked again. It was hard to support his weight on the kicker pedal with the stiff leg, but he repeated the process a second time.

"Are you thinking?"

"Yes."

"Then start it."

Jackson reached down behind the gas tank and turned the key until he heard it click. He put his foot on the kicker pedal and pressed down. He felt the spring tension build on the pedal until it was just right – the most resistance built up from the kicker to the pistons in the motor. And then he lifted himself into the air so that all of his weight was on the pedal of the kicker arm. He kicked it through as hard as he could and twisted the throttle grip as the pedal reached the bottom of its swing.

"Nothing," he said, defeated.

"Why did it not start?" asked the old man. He leaned back in his chair, folded his hands across his lap and threw one ankle up over the opposite knee.

"I don't know," Jackson said. He stared at the bike again. It had a headlight, and a front end, and a gas tank, and a motor, and a transmission, and a pair of wheels, handlebars, there was a cord running from the bars to the dome of the carburetor, a seat, luggage on a sissy bar, and fishtail exhaust pipes that tweeted like a pair of birds when he was going down the road. Jackson stepped forward and twisted the grip of the handlebars again. Inside the cord that ran from the throttle to behind the dome of the carburetor there was a wire cable. Each time he turned the throttle the cable moved. On the carburetor, it was attached to a pivoting mechanism that pushed down a plunger. Running from the other side of the carburetor, a tube stretched through the gap between the heads of the motor and to the petcock on the left side of the gas tank.

"You are on the right track, my friend."

Jackson turned the throttle again and watched the cable pull. And again. The throttle had always worked for him before, from the gas station in Uvalde to the one outside Del Rio, to the city of the river itself where his gas can had fallen off the back of the sissy bar due to his poorly tied knots. It hadn't crossed his mind since then. It is hard to think clearly living a life on the run. The police were coming, and it was entirely likely that they would be there soon if he did not get the bike started. Why had it died in the first place? He was rolling out of Del Rio and then over the Pecos bridge to Langtry where he got drunk in honor of the Honorable Judge Roy Bean and all the heroes of the West that had run that route before Jackson, and then he'd hightailed it out of town and then it stopped running – a lame horse. How did the cowboys bring feed for their steeds with them? The horses must have grazed on the sparse grass that grew when the rains came. Had his steed ate? Had it drank?

Jackson unscrewed the gas cap and nearly dropped it in his frantic. "Oh my Lord."

The old man was laughing in his chair behind Jackson. By the time he turned around to see him, he had his glasses in his hand and was wiping tears from his eyes. "Out of gas my friend!" he howled. Jackson was dumbfounded. "There is a canister around back of the garage. Be careful to not trip on your stiffened leg, we do not want gas to be spilled on the floor!" The old man was still laughing.

Jackson couldn't help but grin as he walked behind the garage. Out of gas! All this trouble because of a few knots and being in such a hurry to go – not too much of a hurry to skip out on a drink of course – which probably made him forget the gas station entirely as he left Langtry. "What the hell am I doing with myself?" he asked with the gasoline sloshing in the canister as he made his way back to the bike.

"The simplest problem you could ever have, my friend!" the old man said as Jackson filled the tank. "You have a beautifully well-maintained old steed. A classic, really. It is the same age as my daughter – a good year. You can set the canister wherever you like, my friend. We will sit and chat a while as the lady makes us supper. She enjoys to cook alone. It clears her mind."

Jackson sat back down in the stool.

No tit-tee motor here that you have got. A real Harley. Panhead! They do not make them like they used to any longer."

"They don't make nothin' like they used to," Jackson said.

"Well that is not true. They are still making old men the same as always! People never change, my friend. Although I suspect that a person does. No, but we old men were always young once. I can remember it like yesterday. I was fresh home from the war in Europe. I bought myself a Harley – Knucklehead. Old military surplus bike. I must have gone everywhere on that thing. I was tanned as leather. So happy always. The war made me that way. What a thing humanity is to need the facing of death to appreciate the lives we can live. In those days it was simple. On the Harley you needed nothing but blue in the sky and calm winds to make for a happy day. It was freedom, my friend. This I am sure you know, but freedom has a way of bringing us back to our place. It seems I rode everywhere."

"Why'd you stop?"

"I have come to the conclusion that all life is a circle. No matter how much you may alter the course, the roads have a way of bringing you back to where you left off from. I am originally from Jalisco, you see? My parents brought me here as a young boy. As bad as the Depression was in America, it was even worse for my people, I think. So we got a fresh start here. My father built this house himself, but he did not have a way with the people. After I went off to war, my parents had none but each other. My mother missed her sisters and her own *madre*. I arrived back from the war in 1945, and they told me they were going home. Home! After fifteen years Jalisco was still their home. I supposed I realized that this was mine after I tried to live my life out there" He gestured to the night through the garage door. "It seems I found my way home too. I married, had a beautiful daughter. I lost my wife only recently. I miss her dearly. But Cynthia looks just like her mother – she has the same charm. She keeps my sanity. One day it may break, but I pray that it does not. I could never live life staring, there is too much out there to see. Ah, and speak of the Devil, this way she comes!"

"You boys about ready for dinner?" She was wearing an apron covered in flour and her brown hair was still pulled tightly back in a ponytail. Both of the men nodded and stood. "Guess you got that ol' thing sorted huh?"

"Yes, yes we did. The young man has done it all himself even."

Jackson nodded. "Guess you could say that."

"Here, let my help you," Cynthia said. She put Jackson's arm around her shoulder and let him rest some of his weight on her as the trio walked to the house. "Daddy, you ever figure out this ol' boy's name?"

"Hmm, no. I suppose I did not even ask. Well, my friend, let us hear your name!"

He was quiet a while, walking stiffly to the front door of the house, resting his weight on the woman's shoulder. "Jackson," he finally said, and he wished he had not. He was not a very good outlaw. He was not good at being on the run. There were too many decisions to be made that were a matter of life and death, or escape. And now these people know exactly who you are, he thought. No alias, no fake name, nothing. You have told them just your real name and so when the police come through town looking for you there will be a person who knows exactly who you are, and in your foolishness now you are sitting at the dinner table with them, you are telling them your real name, that you are from Louisiana, that you worked on a ranch in Uvalde, how you came to own that yellow Panhead even. They are laughing along like it is a funny story. And it is, it is funny that a man like you – as bad an outlaw as you are – it is funny one such as you has even made it this far. But the food is good. And a conversation is so sweet to have after too long spent in your own mind. And how stupid you are to love it, because the old man knows who you are, but he trusts you for some reason, maybe because you *will* him to trust you. Even now, he asks you a question and you have already answered it before it has even run through your mind. You are too *human* to be a great man. You betray yourself at every turn. You are certainly a fool. Why have you told them that you are on the run? Why? Answer yourself why you have betrayed yourself to these people. You wish to break the wheel so much, yet you only want to exist in the comfort that the wheels provide – the smooth ride. You never should have come here. Answer yourself why you betray yourself.

Because this table is what it is to be human.

"Not all bad men are *bad* men," the old man said across the table to Jackson. All of their plates were empty; they leaned back in their chairs casually. The dim yellow lighting of the dining room gave the black-and-white pictures on the wall a sepia tone – almost even colorized them. "An outlaw, even such as yourself, can be a good man. And I believe that you are, but I have no desire to become caught up in your dealings. Keep them away from my home. I hope that you will appreciate my honesty as I have yours."

"I won't bring nothin' around here. Highly unlikely that I ever make my way back here when I'm gone."

"Well don't say that. You never know."

"Yes you do never know, my friend. The road has always a way of bringing you back."

"Maybe so," Jackson said. "But I can't stay here for too long. Runs the risk of gettin' you folks caught up in it."

"I understand that," said the old man.

"There ain't hardly no law presence out here at all. You'll be alright for one night. Take off in the morning, but we'll give you a bed to sleep in. You'll be comfortable."

"I appreciate that. Y'all have done too much for me."

"Nonsense."

"What fun is life if you can't make friends out of strangers?"

Jackson smiled. He stood and started to stack the empty dinner plates.

"Oh, you don't have to do that, honey."

"No. I do. Let me help."

She let him go on stacking the plates. He staggered to the kitchen and washed them under the stove-top light.

"Well, it is time for me to make to bed," the old man said. "I wish you both good night's rest. Jackson Hunter, if I do not see you before you go, make sure to take care of yourself. You *are* a good man, no matter what you may think. Our actions are not all we do in a life. Keep the rubber side down, my friend."

Jackson looked at him from the kitchen and nodded. The old man went off down a hall and Jackson heard the sound of his bedroom door clicking shut. Cindy brought in the final few dishes from the dining room.

"Thank you so much for doing those," she said.

"Don't mention it."

"I never do get much help around here."

"The old man said you don't take to it much."

"Oh, daddy's got a way of thinkin' people don't want no help. Pull yourself up by yer bootstraps and all that, but I suppose it does make us better for it."

"There's a whole lot of ways of lookin' at things."

"Suppose so," she said, picking up a dish towel and drying the plates Jackson had cleaned and set aside. "So why?" she asked after a while, "Why'd you do that old man like that?"

Jackson stopped washing and looked out the window at the twinkling lights of Sanderson in the valley below. "I don't know," he said. "I just wanted a change. Wanted something different in my life, something to look back and think 'holy shit.' You know?"

"I think I do."

"But now all I've really got going through my head is 'What the fuck were you thinking?' Now I'm out here on the lam, and it seems like I can't put no distance between me and what I've done. All those old westerns don't really talk about that shit. You know? Jesse James just takes the money and blows it all in a whore house in Deadwood, or wherever. He don't never have no remorse or nothin'. He's just livin' that life. And so some rich fellas might suffer, but that's ok cause they're rich and all, but it ain't. But here I am now and I feel like I can't turn back and if I keep goin' it's just gonna be draggin' me down all my life."

"Well I don't think you can turn back. I always thought of runnin' off like that, but all that what you just said keeps me grounded. It's a hard thing to do. All that freedom don't come without no baggage to lug about."

"Baggage," Jackson said. "Wish I could just dump it somewhere."

There were new lights moving among those in the valley below. One car came along the highway from town. It was late at night. It drove west on Highway 90 until it passed behind the silhouette of the mountain.

Cindy and Jackson finished the dishes quietly. They were all dried and put away. Cindy held the final chef's knife in her hand. Drying the thick blade carefully and slowly in short circles with the dishtowel. She dropped it on the counter and grabbed Jackson's arm. Her fingers were cold and damp from the towel. "You hear that?" she said.

Jackson cocked his ears and listened, but he heard nothing, just the tinny ringing in his ears. "No."

"I must've imagined it," she said. "Almost like a car running or tires on the gravel."

Jackson felt her fingers slip along his arm as he walked away and through the house to the front door. He peered through the window out into the night and saw nothing. Quietly, he opened the door and stepped out onto the covered front porch and took a few steps further so that he could see the stars. Heavy – oppressing. The powerful stars dangling in beauty there in the heavens – massive enough to remind man that his place is on earth – rooted in mathematical reality that creates all things. The mechanical clicking behind Jackson was almost imperceptible.

※ ※ ※

The Terrell County sheriff had gotten the call that there was a man on the run headed his direction. He was wanted even before he'd stolen all of this money from his ranch owner – he'd slipped the system somehow. But now the guy who'd lost all that money – Hager was his name – was offering a three-thousand-dollar reward to whoever got the money back.

"Three thousand dollars is a lot of money," said the good sheriff. Earlier that day he'd been on patrol and seen Old Man Cardoñez dropping a man off at the Eagle's Nest. The sheriff had thought little of it at the time; Cardoñez was the only Harley mechanic in town, but the yellow motorcycle in the bed of the truck matched the description given out by Uvalde County.

Night had fallen. His shift was supposed to be over soon, but a few hours of overtime could net him enough money to buy any of those new boats he had his eye on, and the bass were biting in Amistad.

He called in to tell Del Rio and Uvalde that he had a lead on the fugitive. He holstered his revolver, shut off the lights in the office and got in his patrol car. They said he needed backup, but you can't share a bass with anyone. He went down Highway 90 alone. It was very late; the stars were shining ominously – as they always do. He turned on to Cardoñez's dirt road and was pleasantly surprised to see the gate left open. No lock cutting necessary. The sheriff drove the car slowly up the dirt road with the lights off. The moon had set, but the night was clear enough for the stars to light the road. He came to a stop just before he crested the top of the hill. He cut the motor, but left the keys in the ignition, got out and left the door open so as to make no noise. On a clear night like this any sound could travel for miles.

He crept slowly off to the right of the driveway. He made a wide arc around the house and could hear the hens cooing softly in their coop. He looked in the garage as he walked past. The motor-cycle was there, and it matched the description per-fectly. He'd found his man.

The sheriff walked slowly and quietly around the back of the house. He could see the stove light on through the kitchen window. Cardoñez's daughter was standing at the sink with her hands on the counter with her head cocked to one side as if she were listening to something very quiet. He could see the bones of her wrist white against the skin. She had the perfect little figure. Nice, tight hips to grab on to. A trim waist. That shimmering brown hair that hung to her shoulders, and that neck with the tendons like buttresses on a church in his cathedral calendar that hung in his of-fice. She had no idea the danger she was in. She'd practically beg him to fuck her after the sheriff saved her. He couldn't wait.

He was rounding the corner of the house now. There was his man, standing there like a statue with his head lolling backwards, staring at the stars. What an idiot.

The sheriff took a quick look up at the little twinkling points of light in the sky. He unholstered his weapon. He cocked the hammer.

Jackson looked over his right shoulder and saw the sheriff. He looked back up at the sky again, and then turned slowly to face the man and the barrel of the pistol pointed between his eyes. The rifling glinted shallowly in the starlight; those little grooves twisted inward to the darkness where the bullet lay in wait.

"You aren't going to shoot me," he said.

"You done hurt a lot of people, Hunter." The pistol was shaking in trembling hands.

Jackson looked back up at the sky. "Yes. Yes I have."

"Now, why don't you just come along with me? You'll answer a few questions – make it all easier for everybody. Nobody gets hurt. You don't scare those nice folks inside."

"And if I fight?"

"Then I am going to shoot you."

"Then I suppose fighting won't do me any good. What about the third option?"

"Which is?"

Jackson looked from the sky back to the sheriff. "You put down that there revolver, I hand you this money in my back pocket, you take it back to Hager, and we call it all even. Nobody gets hurt. You don't scare those nice folks inside."

"You know I can't do that."

Jackson pulled the wad of bills out of his pocket and held them out towards the sheriff.

He looked at them intently. The revolver was dropping to the sheriff's waist, but he raised it again with both arms outstretched and elbows locked. "No."

Jackson pocketed the bills. He looked to the open door of the house. The sheriff sidestepped in an arc so that he was between Jackson and the porch. "You ain't goin' in there," he said. "Now put your hands up where I can see 'em. I'm takin you to town. You're under arrest."

"The good sheriff does his duty," Jackson said. He raised his hands to his head.

"Higher," demanded the sheriff.

Jackson lifted his arms high above him like a child might on the downhill swing of a roller coaster. Over the sheriff's shoulder, he could see

Cynthia peering through the open doorway. She crept through the arch, walking silently and with calculated steps. "So be it."

Cynthia sprung. She stepped to the sheriff like she was hitting the walk-off grand slam in the seventh game of the World Series. Her hands were gripped tightly on the handle of the knife and she slammed the point of the blade into the good sheriff's temple.

Jackson heard the snapping of the metal and the crunch of the man's skull as the blade made impact. The sheriff staggered a few paces to his right, reeling from the blow. He dropped his pistol on the ground and collapsed on top of it. He supported his weight on one elbow. The sharp steel of the broken knife point reflected the stars. Blood was coming from the sheriff's head now. He touched his fingers to the metal at his temple. His mouth was twitching, trying to form the words. The lips convulsing violently. Before he could make sound Cynthia was on him, plunging the jagged knife into his chest again and again. Jackson dropped his arms to his sides.

Now the blood was pooling on the red dirt of West Texas. The sheriff's eyes were open to the oppressing enormity of the night sky. His badge was dented from where the broken knife had hit it. Cynthia was sitting in the dirt, watching the blood pour out. The broken knife was by her side, and the bones of her wrists were covered in the sheriff's blood.

Jackson stood there a while, looking at the scene until the blood had stopped pouring from the wounds in the sheriff's torso. All was still now, and he sat in the dirt too, resting his elbows on his knees, feeling the cold night air press against the cauterized wound on his thigh.

They were silent a long time. Cynthia's eyes were wide. Her shoulders trembled.

"Cindy?"

"Yeah?"

Jackson was quiet.

"Holy shit," she said.

Jackson was quiet, staring at the blood of the man mixing with the dirt.

"Holy shit, I just fucking killed somebody."

The blood reflected the stars too. Jackson threw his head back. He was looking at them for what they were now.

"He had his gun pointed at you – he was...."
She went silent, realizing who he had been.

Jackson looked at her.

She was staring through the sheriff and through the ground to something far, far, impossibly far away.

They were both quiet a long while.

"It ain't no fun," he said. "It ain't no fun feeling that happen. I killed a man once – east of Beaumont. It weren't no fun. I don't even know why I did it. Just to feel what it was like, I guess – to feel all that life slipping away. It's like if you could reach out and grab it, you could stop it. It ain't heavy – I'm sayin'. But slippery – or something like... like a fish in a river.

"I chopped him up, threw him in the Sabine. And I was just settin' there on the bank after I'd thrown what there was of him in the water. Just settin' there, and the sun was startin' to rise. And you know how the sky gets when it does, it just kinda starts to warm like this slow beat of a heart, and then everything seems like it comes to life or somethin'. And I remember hearin' birdsong in the trees, and I remember thinkin' 'How the hell could birds be singin' songs at somethin' like this?' And then they started divin'. They was divin' in the water and snatching up all them little pieces of him, and the fish were swarmin' to him like he was chum.

"And *oh God* I made him to be that. From a *man* to *that*. But the world just did not care. It just kept on goin." His voice faltered, but his eyes were still firm. "The world just don't care what kinda life you live, or it don't care what you are neither. The world just goes. And them birds was just singin' to the sunrise – singin' to the new day like it was no different from yesterday. But they wasn't singin' when the sun set. And you can make your life however you want to make it, but they won't sing to that either. And the world won't care no matter how much you try to change it. It's just gonna keep on going. Time don't matter. No where, no when. The world just keeps turnin' under all those stars and everything we men do here only matters to us men. It don't make no difference at all to the world. And that's just the way it works. The birds are gonna be singin' when the sun comes up on the last day, and the day after that too. They didn't lament when Jesus died, or Caesar, or Billy the Kid neither. They don't know no eras or change that we think of. It's

117

just the air, and the trees, and the worms in the dirt, and the dawning of a new day is all."

Then he looked back up at the stars, and it was as though the sudden confession over the dead man had brought his sins to him. He remembered the young man. He'd followed him for weeks, stabbed him with a pen knife through the eyes. His screams. Hands on a bloody throat. Silence. He took him home. He took a chainsaw to the corpse. He loaded the bits up in buckets. The birds had sung when he tossed them in the river. The sun rising. The frantic fleeing through the forest. Home, in his bed. The banging on the locked bedroom door. First his mother. Then his father. The police. The cuffing. The blood in the garage. The wails of his mother in court. Then the guiding him to the car and the drive through the countryside. The Newton Mental institution. A worn-down old church. Rotting wood floors. Dopey stares from the others. The bed. Worn and lumpy. Television. *The television playing Gunsmoke. Playing Gunsmoke. Playing Gunsmoke.* A temporary escape. Then solitude.

The bed there and the strapped arms and the always facing upward to the rotting wood boards of the ceiling. The voice. "You've hurt a lot of people Mr. Hunter, Why?" The shocking. The electricity. "Now why can't you just answer a few simple questions Mr. Hunter?" Electricity. *Gunsmoke* – please. "Just make this easier for everybody." The struggling against the straps. The rotting wood of the ceiling. Where was the sky? "Mr. Hunter, I'm going to have to keep shocking you if you cannot cooperate." Where were the stars? Let me go! "You know I can't do that." The resistance. "I'm going to have to shock you again Mr. Hunter, please cooperate." The electricity. The tightening of the muscles. The clenching of the jaw and the frothing of his mouth. "Higher." Limp. "That is enough. Shut it down. I will be back to talk with you again tomorrow, Mr. Hunter."

The clang of the closing door. Then the rotting wood of the ceiling. Then utter darkness. Where were the stars? Where was the sky? There must be some sky. There must be some blue in the sky. The rotting wood of the ceiling. The struggle. The violent struggle against the straps. And then the escape. Yes, there must have been the escape. Why could he not remember the escape? There must have been the escape. There must have been the climbing out of the bed. The sprint through crowded hallways. The *Gunsmoke* theme song playing on the televisions. The casting of the doors aside. *Gunsmoke.* Yes, the escape. There must have been the running through fields. The hiding from the dogs in the underbrush. The clothing store. The train station. The ranch. The ranch. *Gunsmoke.* The electricity. The running. The money. Yes there must have been the escape. The wind. The wind. The wind. The tweeting of the birds. The fluttering freedom. There must have been the escape. There must have been. There must have been the escape. There must have been the escape. *There must have been the escape.* There was the escape – the sky.

Cynthia was looking at the stars, Jackson was too. She looked at him, he at her. The green of her eyes in the fading darkness. Then they looked back to the sky and the oppressive weight and ominousness of the cosmos was being swept away by the slow creeping of the dawn – day after day it was. Days pass like dust in the wind – light – airy – even weightless. Every day. Eternity after eternity.

"I wonder if the stars ever change."

They were both quiet a while, watching the stars slowly fade away as the light eased up over the horizon line to the east and seeped into the brilliant night sky. First a faint yellow, then the fluorescent orange. And then suddenly – that simple shade of blue.

"I wonder if men do."

※ ※ ※

Jackson pulled the bills from his pocket. He set them on the ground beside Cindy. "Get washed up," he told her.

She just looked at him and nodded.

"Tell 'em it was me. Tell 'em I forced you into helpin'."

She nodded again.

"And then go. Wake up one mornin' and decide that the life you're livin' ain't the one you want to live any more. The old man'll be fine. We all need to go someplace sometimes. It helps us find home."

He limped away from her slowly in the still morning air. He could hear the birds singing shrill

121

songs in their nests. The stallion was sitting in the stable, its yellow mane unmoving in the morning air. He breathed it in – that sweet breath of a new day. A good day where yesterday no longer mattered. All there was to do was ride – ride as far as you like and wherever you like and if you don't like the way that you're headed then you can wake up the next morning and start out anew all over again. *That's the beauty of it,* and the steed was ready. Make sure to feed her. Let her keep her energy up. You will learn the shoeing and the maintenance of the hooves as it comes to you. But now all there is to do is ride her. That's what she was made for. Is it not?

He put his foot in the stirrup and cranked the kicker pedal slowly. Caressing the golden mane with one hand, he twisted the throttle twice with the other. He kicked it through. And then he repeated the process. The click, click, click of the kicker ratcheting up the compression. And then the kick – the harsh singing of the birds from the exhaust that joined the song from the morning air around him.

He sat in the saddle and listened. He breathed in another deep breath of the crisp beginning of a new day. He slid his aviators on his face.

His jacket was unbuttoned, but it is good to feel some cold on your chest from time to time.

Cindy had gone inside the house. The body of the sheriff lay in a pool off muddy coagulated blood, and the shard of the knife in his skull shone like a star under the pale sunlight.

Jackson tapped the Panhead down into first gear. The motor hummed low as he pulled away from the house. He putted past the parked squad car. He could hear the clicking of the transmitter inside. The rocks behind the car were vibrant red against the pale blue of the sky. You must never forget this sky, he told himself. And then he tore away from the place.

He flew down the mountain with the motor roaring loudly – the bike near impossible to keep upright over the rocks and the shifting sand beneath. There were more police coming up the road with their lights flashing red and blue. They saw him and stopped. Some of the officers got out of their cars and hid behind the doors with their guns drawn.

Jackson twisted the throttle farther and the bike roared between the vehicles, and he could hear the shouts of the policemen and the sheriffs. Then the reports of their guns. He could see the dust swirling all around them when he looked over his shoulder, their pistols flashing, and his tires churned through the dirt, and he heard the cracking of the pistols and then the growling of engines as the police turned their cars around to chase him, tires turning, adding their own dust to his. It all plumed softly into the air in a ruddy cloud above the slope of the mountain.

He turned west once more onto Highway 90 and looked back. There hung that huge cloud of red dust stark against the unending blue of the morning sky. Soon the motor was singing and the road was rushing beneath him again. The sun warmed his back, and he could feel the cold wind on his chest. Jackson Hunter was smiling.

About the Author

Born in 1994 and raised in the Hill Country of Central Texas, Warren Stoddard II attended Texas State University in San Marcos and there fell in love with early-model Harley-Davidsons. Following his graduation from Texas State, he travelled to Syria to join the YPG, a Kurdish militia, and was later wounded in action liberating the city of Ash Sha'fah from ISIS control. He now lives in Birmingham, Alabama with his wife and dog.

His short literary work has been featured in *DicE Magazine*, *Into the Void*, *The Barely South Review*, *Smut Butt's Freaky Fiction*, and numerous other publications. This is his first book.

warrenstoddard.com